KILLING
CONFIDENCE

ABOUT THE AUTHOR

Matt Bendoris has worked in the newspaper industry since 1989 when he began writing a pop column for the *Glasgow Guardian*. He soon made the leap into national titles before moving to London where he was hired twice by Piers Morgan. Matt first worked under Piers at the *Sun* before joining the showbiz team at the *Mirror* under Morgan's editorship. There he became deputy to Matthew Wright, currently a morning host on the Five TV channel.

In 1996 he returned to Scotland as Chief Feature Writer for the *Scottish Sun* where he continues to interview subjects from celebrities and politicians to the occasional serial killer. During that time he ghost-wrote two autobiographies, the Krankies' *Fan-Dabi-Dozi* and *Simply Devine: The Sydney Devine story*.

When his office was relocated to Glasgow city centre, Matt began commuting by train and wrote *Killing with Confidence* on his battered old BlackBerry to pass the time on the short journey between Croy and Queen Street station. He lives in Kilsyth with his wife Amanda and their two children Andrew and Brooke.

KILLING WITH CONFIDENCE

MATT BENDORIS

THE CRIME LAB

This edition published 2013
by The Crime Lab, an imprint of Books Noir

Copyright © 2013 Matt Bendoris

All Rights Reserved

ISBN 978 1 904684 83 1

A CIP record for this book is available from the British Library

Typeset in Garamond by Park Productions

Cover design by James Hutcheson

Cover picture copyright: Paul Gooney/Arcangel Images

Printed and bound in the EU

DEDICATION

To Amanda, for always believing in me and
Andrew and Brooke for making it all worthwhile.
My mum, for raising my brother Sean and I on her own,
Bob for getting me over the finishing line and my beloved
colleague Yvonne, for all her assistance.
This book is in memory of Danny Brown, my first, and
best editor, mentor and friend.

EPIGRAPH

Osiris – one of the most important gods of ancient Egypt. The origin of Osiris is obscure; he was a local god of Busiris in Lower Egypt and may have been a personification of chthonic (underworld) fertility, or possibly a deified hero. By about 2,400 BC, however, Osiris clearly played a double role: he was both a god of fertility and the embodiment of the dead and the resurrected …

CONTENTS

OSIRIS

Growing up in the post-war shipping port of Hull in England's North East had been tough. Being called Osiris made it even tougher. Osiris Vincent Vance endured ridicule and exclusion from his first day at school. Even his primary teacher had mocked his unusual name, to the squeals of delight from the rest of the class.

From that moment on Osiris was an outsider. In later years he changed his name to Vinnie, but it made little difference. He would always be Osiris in Hull.

He was named after an entry his mum Veronica had found in the *Encyclopaedia Britannica*, which she had unsuccessfully tried to sell on almost every doorstep around the historical city.

She'd been heavily pregnant at the time and lugging those impossibly heavy books had left her with ugly-looking varicose veins covering her legs. She was just nineteen years old.

Her first and only lover had been a merchant seaman, who promised her the earth, then disappeared as soon as her waist began to thicken. He'd known she was pregnant long before the naïve teenager did.

Veronica's parents ordered an abortion. They knew someone who performed them. Not a doctor, of course. It was 1947, the year before the National Health Service had been formed, and they could afford neither his fee nor the shame it would bring on the family.

The abortion had been bloody, painful, and as it turned out unsuccessful. Her belly continued to grow. As Veronica spent weeks recovering from the botched procedure, she read the encyclopaedias. She didn't understand many of the big words or explanations. But one entry leapt out: *Osiris … both a god of fertility and the embodiment of the dead and resurrected.*

'That's him alright.' She knew it was a boy. A boy whose life they had tried to take. But he had survived, resurrected from the dead. This baby was going to be born no matter what and he would leave his mark on this world, of that she was certain.

BLACK & BLUE

April Lavender wiped her mouth clean of the flour dust from her morning sausage roll, sprinkled with a liberal helping of salt and smothered in brown sauce. At lunchtime she would return for a cheese and ham roll washed down with whatever soup the Peccadillo café had to offer, which she also routinely salted before tasting. She couldn't get her head round this new low salt way of thinking. She knew of some younger colleagues who didn't even take salt on their chips. 'How could anyone eat chips without salt?' she muttered a little too loudly to herself, earning a sideways glance from a taxi driver at a neighbouring table.

No, April was too old to change her ways at fifty-six. She loved salt on her food and had the high blood pressure to prove it. Anyway she'd given up trying to be healthy since modern science seemed determined to take away everything she enjoyed. Recently it had reported that bacon shouldn't be eaten at all and any alcohol shortened your life dramatically. If that was the case it was a wonder she was still breathing.

At least April had managed to quit one vice, smoking, after the birth of her first grandchild last year – spurred on by the cruel ultimatum from her daughter that the baby wouldn't be allowed to stay over unless Granny stopped her forty-a-day habit.

'The cheek of her,' April mumbled, 'I have to stop smoking so she can get a babysitter.'

The taxi driver shifted uncomfortably in his seat before deciding to pay up and leave in case April tried to strike up a conversation with someone other than herself.

Unfortunately, since the fags had gone April had piled on the weight. Nothing fitted any more. Last week she had to suffer the indignity of her blouse button pinging off and landing on a colleague's desk, to much hilarity around the office. Her humiliation was complete when she was forced to cover up her decency by stapling her shirt back together.

It hadn't always been this way. Back in her teens she'd been a real looker. Long blonde hair – not the harsh dye job it was now to cover the grey – shapely legs and a pert bust that sent the fellas wild.

She had settled down with a tall, charming, handsome man, who soon turned into a pot-bellied pig. They stumbled on for five years, producing two children, before she finally had enough, left him and moved back in with her folks. The next few years had been tough. Her ex had refused to pay a penny for the kids. 'How do these buggers expect their children to survive?' she'd often say to anyone who'd listen. Conditions were cramped beyond belief in her ageing parents' tiny bungalow.

April was also what was termed an 'unskilled worker'. But after a secretarial night class, she got a job on a local paper, the *Weekly Extra*, based on the Southside of Glasgow. She was the editor's secretary and loved it. She could never understand why secretaries all wanted to be called personal assistants these days. She'd been proud of her title.

April loved the paper and in particular loved speaking to readers. Even if they called with a complaint she could usually soothe them over without having to bother the boss. People trusted her. They would tell her things that even merited reports in the paper. April hated handing these tips over to the surly journalists, who were more interested in filing their expenses – the most inventive work they produced all week – than filing copy for the paper. They usually made a pig's ear of the stories, anyway, especially if there was a human interest angle rather than just the formulaic court reporting.

One day April convinced her editor to allow her to write a story of her own. The reporters were outraged and complained to the National Union of Journalists. It was the early 1980s and the whole country was gripped by the miners' strike and recession. It seemed as if every affiliated union was just itching to join in – including the three reporters at the *Extra* who were determined to keep a closed shop. They only backed down when the editor promised that his secretary wouldn't be paid for her work and it would appear under the by-line of 'April Lavender – guest writer'.

That seemed to placate them for a while. The truth is, April didn't care about the journalists' sensitivities. She knew she had that all-important foot in the door. Every week her articles would appear, taking up more and more space and shoving stories by the 'proper' journalists into the margins. They resented her, especially when the postbag was full of mail addressed to April. But their resentment turned to outright hatred when five years later she leapfrogged them all to land the post of editor.

Editor. Pride coursed through her body every morning when she read that sign on her office door. The money was okay, but it was the prestige she adored more. She was a pillar of the local community. Just a year later she made another leap, into the nationals, tripling her meagre wage. She had been with the *Daily Herald* now for nearly twenty years. But the energy and ambition that had once driven her out of a doomed marriage and perpetual poverty was fading.

April had a new boss who didn't like her. The Weasel was always sending her copy back to be rewritten. That had never happened to her before – in the local newspaper days she had been the one who sent articles back to be redone. And today she'd learned of a new humiliation. She was being shunted sideways, from women's editor to the newly created Special Investigations desk.

The problem was that her newspaper spent little time and resources on proper investigations now. It was the same throughout the industry. Even the world famous *Sunday Times* Insight team had been disbanded. And she would still have to report to the Weasel. Why didn't they just say what it really was? One foot out the door.

EU laws made it so much more difficult for employers to get rid of their workforce these days. But give someone a new job then three months later tell them it wasn't working out and they could still boot you onto the street.

Yip, three months was all she reckoned she had left. Then what? She still had a crippling mortgage, car and all the other bills to pay.

She needed that salary, especially since there was only one income now after her third marriage collapsed during one almighty row last Christmas. April felt depressed. She was in desperate need of some comfort food and asked the waitress to add a bacon roll to her bill as well.

Half an hour late April tottered in her high heels towards the office. New day, new desk, new colleague, new career. 'Who am I kidding?' thought April. 'More like the end of an old one.'

A wave of dread swept over April as she thought, 'There's no place for an old hack like me any more.' She stared at the ground and noticed something wasn't quite right. 'Oh, great, odd shoes.' Sure enough, her footwear was identical in style, but very different shades. April waddled slowly to the entrance of her work full of misery. What a state she was in.

And she had a point, what with her peroxide blonde hair blowing in the wind, an ample behind swinging from side to side and her bust straining at her blouse. But it was her shoes that would have caught the attention of a more observant passer-by. In the daylight one was black, the other clearly blue.

THE MOTIVATOR

Osiris used to be sloppy when it came to his nocturnal activities, as he now thought of them.

He'd nearly been captured several times, usually because he was blind drunk when he did what he liked to do with prostitutes. Once he was caught literally red-handed – hands dripping in blood from a hooker he'd just strangled to death. The problem was she'd haemorrhaged from both her nose and mouth, sending great spurts of the stuff all over his arms, face and body. Her screams had alerted a neighbour, who broke down the door, and Osiris had only escaped by leaping head first through the first-floor window. He still bore a three-inch scar running along his hairline from the shattered window-pane.

That had been a long time ago in Gateshead, but he'd got markedly better at his nocturnal activities after becoming addicted to self-help tapes. They were marvellous motivators: how to be better at what you do, how to feel good about yourself, how to plan your steps then set about achieving every one of your goals. Most of all they gave him the confidence he had lacked all his life. They had added a degree of professionalism to his work, turning him from a violent, drunken murderer into a cold-blooded killer.

Now he could appreciate and savour every moment of the kill, instead of waking up the next day with a sore head and covered in whores' blood. Yes, these self-help tapes, and later CDs, had transformed his life, making him examine himself, his very foundations, to truly understand what made him tick.

After a long period of soul searching he had come to the conclusion that nothing made him tick at all. The only thing that 'juiced him up' – a phrase from one of the American gurus he listened to avidly – was killing.

As far as Osiris had been concerned he wasn't crazy. 'How can I be?' he'd chortle to himself. 'I've held down jobs all my life, married, raised a family, killed and killed and killed and never been caught. That's not madness – that's genius.'

His job allowed him to be a 'commuting killer', which meant he was able to put hundreds of miles between himself and his crime. The problem was avoiding detection. There was no doubt the police had his DNA profile in their database. No matter how careful the crime and how much protection he used, from condoms to surgical gloves, advances in forensic technology meant that every contact with a victim left behind a trace – and therefore clues – of some sort.

CCTV was Osiris's other enemy. They were next to useless for preventing a 'live crime' – with an estimated 100,000 cameras in operation around Britain, it would be impossible for their operators to monitor them all – but they were the perfect crime-fighting tool to trace criminals after the event. They also provided evidence for their court trials afterwards.

Osiris was lucky that with the high mileage of his job he was able to change company cars frequently. Osiris would make sure each new car was a different colour, make and model from the last one. 'I think I'd like a red Mondeo this time,' was his running joke with Isabel in accounts.

'What are you like?' she would say with mock annoyance. 'Most of the other managers stick with the same models, but not you, Vinnie, always looking to try something different.'

'Ain't that the truth,' he'd say with a wink.

Osiris even impressed himself the way he was able to integrate and communicate with normal members of society, given he had started life as an outsider and felt anything but normal. In times of quiet reflection he would compare himself to an alcoholic. 'Why do alcoholics drink? Because they love it. That's me. I kill because I love killing. No more, no less.'

The self-help gurus had helped Osiris find the clarity he craved. In his world he was no longer the outsider, but a god. He was a God of Fertility. He knew this to be true. He had only had sex with his wife a handful of times throughout an unhappy ten-year marriage and she had fallen pregnant almost every time. He was also a God of the Dead – the body count left behind lay testament to that. And he was a God of the Resurrected. His grandparents had tried to terminate his life when he was still inside the womb, but had failed. A crime they later paid for with their lives.

It was the self-help tapes which had made him realise that. They hadn't even told him anything he didn't know already, but they had given him the tools to work it all out, or as he called it, the 'almighty kick up the backside' needed to achieve his one and only ambition. To be the biggest serial killer in British history.

A SECRET AFFAIR

While April was tucking into her second roll of the morning, Selina Seth unbuckled the seat belt of the Aston Martin V8 Vantage, unzipped her passenger's trousers and sank her head into his lap.

They were taking one hell of a risk meeting like this in broad daylight, but it was worth it. For she had in her mouth a man of power. Married, of course, but then again so was she. God, how she loved its shape, its sleekness, its thrust. Of course, she'd always loved fast cars. Her first had been a Ford Fiesta. How many times had she given head in that old banger? Too many times to remember. But this was different. This was a man and a vehicle of status.

She had always been popular with the boys, growing up in Balornock in the North of Glasgow. There weren't many Selinas around there, that's for sure. With a name like that, a mane of natural blonde hair and eventually sprouting to almost six feet in height, she literally stood head and shoulders above the locals growing up in one of the most deprived areas in the country.

And no one had been more determined to leave the poverty behind than she. Sure, Selina had the looks, but she was street smart enough to know that looks would only get you so far. So, she went into sales, where she excelled, working in everything from advertising to the retail industry.

She loved the sharp suits, her first company car the patter and the wheeling and dealing. But most of all she loved power. The power that came with promotion. The power that came with blowing the boss. Funny how even the biggest boardroom bruiser would melt with the ancient art of fellatio. Such a simple act, too.

Now she had her own company – Seth International – selling jewellery direct to people's homes. But not just ordinary jewellery. Oh no, her jewellery was endorsed by celebrities. She was at home in the shallow showbiz scene. Combine that with the fakes of the fashion world and she was in her element. Her most recent celebrity acquisition had been Dannii Minogue, sister of Australian superstar Kylie. She had of course wanted Kylie, but 'her people' had proved too difficult to deal with and in the end had simply asked for too much money – one million to be exact for just one photo shoot and an endorsement that would last only six months. They also wanted fifty per cent of the profits. Selina would have had to shift a lot of necklaces to recoup that sort of outlay.

Her husband Martin, the brains behind the business, deliberately kept himself in the shadows, allowing his glamorous missus to hog the limelight. But when it came to money, he held the purse strings, and in the end he'd vetoed the Kylie deal. Selina had reluctantly acquiesced, after nearly bankrupting their company the previous year signing up the winner from the *Big Brother* series. How was Selina to know that everyone would have forgotten this so-called celebrity before the advertising campaign had even kicked off?

Her husband now refused to pay over the odds for 'star names', citing that they did nothing for sales, anyway. For Seth International's biggest market was in fact gaudy, chunky gold jewellery, the sort favoured by female football fans that usually spelled out their names – presumably in case they forgot them after too many Bacardi Breezers.

Selina shivered at the thought that she, a friend to the stars, had actually made her fortune selling tat. That's why she craved the celebrity front so much. The truth is she wanted to be a celebrity, too, and in a way she was. Well, sort of. People would stop and stare when she was out and about. She had once even been mistaken for Penny Lancaster. So what if Rod Stewart's latest wife was hardly A-list material, the fact that Selina looked like someone famous was what counted. It meant she had an air about her that separated her from the riff-raff.

As Selina allowed her mind to wander, her illicit lover reached his climax. The voyeur in a nearby car with darkened rear windows was busy pleasuring himself as he watched their tryst in the remote car park at the edge of Strathclyde Country Park. You couldn't actually see the act itself, but it was clear what was going on with that blonde mane of hair in motion and the man's face contorted with pleasure.

Shortly afterwards, Selina's lover left her after a long, lingering farewell kiss. The tall blonde stepped out of his car and waved goodbye as the Aston Martin sped off. The voyeur unlocked his door and wondered to himself if this attractive-looking blonde fancied some seconds ...

ALL SHOOK UP

The *Daily Herald* was situated on Albion Street at the north end of Glasgow city centre. At one time there had been four newspapers in the vicinity. Warehouses and factories had made way for tapas bars and fine dining restaurants, making the once thriving journalists' haunt, the Press Bar, look distinctly tawdry.

April felt a bit like the pub – she was the product of a bygone era. Now she'd learned she was to be teamed up with some young buck from the news desk. She had seen him around, but they'd never really spoken. She'd never wanted to. He was so sure of himself, strutting about like he owned the place. Strange, him being dumped with her. She'd thought he was one of the paper's high-fliers. A favoured one. Maybe he was being sent over to spy on her, to confirm what her bosses already believed, that she was past it. Great, another snake in the grass. She just knew they wouldn't get on.

The 'snake in the grass' had been christened Connor Presley but would spend his life being called Elvis. It had followed him all the way from school through the doors of his local newspaper where he'd started as a teenage apprentice. Even his own mother called him Elvis. His attempts to label himself with a cooler variation – The King – had been in vain. However, one advantage of being nicknamed after the king of rock'n'roll was the kudos it gave Connor within Scotland's substantial crime community – an invaluable commodity as chief crime reporter on Scotland's largest newspaper. Anyone who's anyone in the crime world has a cool nickname. Adam 'The Axeman' Alexander. 'Two Shooters' Sheridan. Or one of his personal favourites, Barry 'The Butcher' Butcher, given to him without the slightest hint of irony by Glasgow's Godfather, who out of a mixture of fear, loathing and respect was simply called Mr Ferguson.

The other advantage of being called Elvis was that *all* of the underworld were as passionate about the King as they were about making money. The American Mafia could keep their Sinatra, as far as Scottish criminals were concerned. In fact, it was rumoured people had been killed in Glasgow just for trying to compare the two.

In Barry 'The Butcher' Butcher's council house, pride of place over his mantelpiece, was a bronze portrait of the King from his chubby Las Vegas era. After suffering decades of accumulated nicotine layers left by Barry's chain-smoking ninety-year-old mum Jessie, you could just about make out the words 'Gone – but not forgotten' inscribed below the King's bloated neck. With Barry's infamous temper, visitors were well advised to enthusiastically appraise his favourite piece of Elvis 'art' – preserved for eternity by the tar from a million of Jessie's Benson & Hedges. Connor always made sure to remark, 'That picture's fucking magic, Barry,' each and every time he visited.

This was Connor's calling in life. Sure, he had to deal with scumbags, but it was a fact of life that their stories sold newspapers. Connor called it 'West of Scotland showbiz' for a country that lacked truly big showbiz stars – Sean Connery, Ewan McGregor, James McAvoy and Billy Connolly the exceptions to the rule. But it was more than made up for with a thriving underworld scene. Ironically, it had been covering this sparse showbiz scene where Connor had first made his name. He was not afraid of ruffling feathers and he had trampled over the cosy relationships the country's actors and TV personalities had enjoyed with his predecessors.

As a kid he'd voraciously read as many papers as he could get his hands on and had come to understand the different tales favoured by certain newspapers and their political leanings. He'd had no time for school. He couldn't be bothered learning the periodic table when he was more interested in what was making the headlines that morning. Although bright, his grades suffered as a result.

Fortunately, he wanted to be part of an industry where lack of qualifications was never an inhibitor. His first editor Danny Brown had once laughed, 'Qualifications? Kelvin MacKenzie was the most famous Fleet Street editor of modern times and he only had one O-level. I've seen young, so-called journalists qualify from universities top of their class who wouldn't know a good story if it came up and bit them on the arse. Reporting isn't something you can be taught. It's an instinct – and you've got it.'

After four years pricking giant-sized egos on the showbiz scene Connor was called in to his editor's office and told he would be replacing Badger on the news desk. Russell 'Badger' Blackwood, the country's longest-serving and most legendary crime reporter, was about to take an unwanted early retirement.

'But Russell covers crime,' Connor protested.

'I know that,' barked the editor, 'but I need someone to replace him before he drinks himself to death or strokes out on me. The change will do you good. Add some strings to your bow.'

So, Connor was placed under the supervision of Badger, who had spent his entire career crafting exclusives and his most distinguished feature, a large, veiny, purple whisky-drinker's nose. He had greeted Connor on his first day with, 'So, you're the cunt after my job,' but from then on the pair miraculously hit it off. Badger's job was to take Connor round all his police and crime contacts to show him the ropes.

Basically, it was one big booze-up that lasted for about three months. Badger would arrange to meet Connor in pubs down Glasgow's old Fruitmarket, sometimes at seven in the morning, where they'd enjoy a 'breakfast pint' with market workers and postmen at the end of their shifts, all on the pretence of meeting some valuable underworld contact. When the mysterious contact failed to show – presumably because they were still in bed – they would try to source him out, which meant drifting in and out of pubs in Glasgow's East End for the rest of the day.

Occasionally, when they did actually bump into some of the crime world's hierarchy it seemed to come as much as a shock to Badger as it did to Connor. These occasions meant even more drink and late nights, with Badger telling whoever would listen, 'You can trust Elvis as if he was my own fucking son,' followed by Badger demanding a version of 'Blue Suede Shoes'.

But at the end of the initial binging, amazingly, Connor had actually made some huge strides in his new field and managed to file some pretty impressive page leads about 'hits' which had been ordered between rival gangs, drug shipments which had been lost by the cops, and even his first exclusive crime splash – front page – on an underworld boss who was getting married to one of his fiercest rivals' daughters. That had crime reporters in other papers desperately scrambling around the day after for follow-ups, leaving Connor with a smug, satisfied feeling inside.

But he knew his old mentor Badger was a dinosaur who was about to become extinct. In Connor's short career he could see how reporting had changed out of all recognition in the last decade. The unions had long been crushed and left toothless, and with them old-school reporters like Badger, who would merrily drink their way through morning, noon and night shifts, at the same time hoovering up all the best scoops. He was making way for a new breed of clean-living, ultra-professional 'millennium reporters', as Badger once called them, adding, 'Boring bastards, too, each and every one of them.'

These new reporters certainly couldn't match Badger for stories – personally or professionally. He told of a sports reporter who turned up a week late for work, the worse for drink, with a shotgun. Surprisingly, this hadn't sent his colleagues cowering in terror. Instead, the sports editor shouted across the office, 'Is that thing loaded?' 'I don't know,' replied the sozzled reporter, swaying gently from side to side. 'Well, find out,' replied his boss, which he promptly did – by blasting the door to the editor-in-chief's office clean off its hinges. This had happened many years before Connor's arrival, but Badger swore the editor-in-chief emerged from his gunsmoke-filled room and calmly asked, 'Who's there?'

The reporter's nicknames were fantastic, too. Besides Badger, who earned his moniker because he would badger someone relentlessly until they told him the story, there was the Bucket, thus named because of the heroic quantities of drink he could sink – in an industry drowning in alcohol quite a claim, although it never affected his ability to work, or drive home for that matter.

Connor's personal favourite was the Brick, named not because he was a particularly big, hard chap, but because he kept a solid brick in the top drawer of his desk. This was only discovered when he removed it and threatened to brain a little fusspot from payroll who had innocently forgotten his wages one Friday afternoon – in the days when journalists received weekly pay packets.

Connor had enjoyed a stint as a showbiz reporter working for Piers Morgan on the *Sun*'s Bizarre column in London in the 1990s. He'd loved Piers's cheeky style of writing; how he could gently take the Mickey out of subjects he liked and absolutely slaughter those he didn't. It was something Connor took with him when he moved into crime reporting, and it hadn't taken Connor long to spot the similarities between celebrities and organised criminals.

First, just about all of them do drugs – great, huge snortfuls of the stuff. Second, they're both relatively young and rich, with fortunes no decent working person would ever come close to. And, finally, they all love being in the newspapers. While most celebrities claimed this wasn't the case, and he'd often read of some starlet bleating on about 'press intrusion', Connor knew that take away the intrusion and they'd be complaining that no one was interested in them any more. Quite simply, they wanted stories written about their latest squeeze or movie role – anything that added to their image and kept them in the spotlight.

But the most striking similarity between the showbiz and criminal worlds, Connor knew, was that for the most part they both had extremely short careers, the major difference being that while the stars drifted out of favour, the criminals were likely to come a cropper thanks to a lengthy prison sentence – or dying a very violent death.

But in the last week, Connor's life had been turned on its head.

Without warning, his editor Danny Brown had taken early retirement – or was 'kicked out on his arse', as he candidly told his staff – to make way for Nigel Bent, an Englishman who clearly didn't see the editorship of the *Daily Herald* as the pinnacle of his career, merely a stepping-stone to greater things. Of course, the problem with using a job as a stepping-stone is that you tend to step on a lot of people, too.

Badger had been the first casualty, dismissed with a pay cheque before the new editor had even taken the chair. Human Resources had obviously had their eyes on Badger for a long time, but Danny

Brown had protected him. Without that shield, they thanked him for forty years of service, misspelled his surname as 'Blackdood' on his farewell letter, and told him to clear his desk immediately.

Connor was next to be swept aside after the new broom Bent announced during conference one morning that his 'pet hate' was gangster stories. Once an editor made a public declaration like that, there was no going back. So, gangsters, thugs and criminals would be sidelined, along with Connor whose job it was to report them. He was summarily dispatched to a new special investigations unit with April Lavender, a batty old bird whom he'd heard had a drink problem.

AN ENTHUSIASTIC AMATEUR

Osiris had been highly critical of his fellow killer. The attack was certainly violent enough, but way too scrappy. Too emotional. The attacker had failed to distance himself from the victim and as a result the frenzied assault was over too quickly.

Unable to help himself he spoke out loud, 'Slow it down. Savour the moment.'

The attacker froze. Osiris cursed his own stupidity.

Seconds later the murderer was gone, speeding off in his car. Osiris moved in to inspect the recently deceased. She was tall, blonde and beautiful. He snapped on a pair of surgical gloves he always kept to hand in his car and lifted the vic's head and laughed out loud. 'That's why it was over so quickly, you broke her neck.' He sighed. 'What a bloody novice. What a bloody waste.' He made his way back to his red Mondeo.

Like the blonde's killer, Osiris had also been watching her have sex in the Aston Martin. He liked to trawl discreet car parks around the country where, as a voyeur, you could usually spot some illicit affairs going on. Occasionally, he'd got lucky himself when he was asked to join in – dogging, as it was called in the tabloid press.

Osiris had watched as the blonde and her would-be killer had a brief conversation. From her demeanour it seemed as if she knew her attacker. Whatever she said made him fly into a violent rage. She hadn't even had the chance to defend herself such was the ferocity of the attack.

Osiris now needed to focus. He needed his self-help tapes. 'Channel your energy,' the American voice intoned. 'Remember, knowledge is power.'

Fate had handed Osiris a crucial piece of information. He now just had to figure out how to use it.

A BROOM WITH A VIEW

The Weasel took great delight in showing April and Connor their new Special Investigations office, which had until a day ago been a broom cupboard where the cleaners kept their mops and Hoovers, and by the smell of things, also enjoyed illicit cigarettes.

'Here we are – the hub,' the Weasel sneered. 'The ideas factory, call it what you will, but the company has gone to a lot of time and effort to set this up, so we expect results.'

The Weasel had been rehearsing his sarcastic little speech after snorting up a thick five-inch line of cocaine through a rolled-up twenty-pound note. He'd never normally needed such a big hit so early in the morning. This new job of his was the loftiest position of his career, however, an impartial observer may have concluded that he was way out of his depth. But such ambitious people never realise it.

April's instincts had been right about the Weasel. He did want rid of her. Part of his long-term game plan was to find a job for his mistress, who was presently working for a struggling Edinburgh news agency. That way he'd be able to co-ordinate their affair more effectively. At present, he struggled to recall the last time they'd 'done it.' He couldn't even remember when they'd shared a line of coke.

But staff jobs these days were hard to come by. Even when a journalist retired or was fired, desk heads struggled to replace them as the newspaper circulations continued their terminal downward spiral – especially if the outgoing staff received huge pay-offs. The Weasel had pleaded a very convincing case to his editor Nigel Bent to install his lover in April's place and promised to get rid of the 'old dear on the cheap'. With his mistress in place this would also allow him to spy on Connor, who, as far as the Weasel was concerned, needed bringing down a peg or two. He'd been the blue-eyed boy for too long.

The Weasel's real name was Gordon McGillivray. Throughout his career he had been the complete antithesis of a blue-eyed boy, with his greasy lank hair, skinny frame, red and perpetually dripping nose, sharp facial features and unfortunate halitosis, which his staff would get an unwelcome lungful of whenever he stood too close or bollocked them.

He'd always resented Connor's type – the show ponies of newspapers – and instead had connived and backstabbed his way into power. It also helped that he knew something about his editor that no one else did. He'd hinted as much to Bent, who received and understood his news editor's intentions when the topic had moved to retaining April's staff position for a 'newer, younger, cheaper … and more attractive female reporter.'

So, April Lavender was not being paranoid. Her days were numbered. Soon the Weasel would be back in the arms of his lover – the only person he knew who enjoyed cocaine as much as he did.

'I'll leave you two to get to know each other – but no shagging in here, please, we've just had the place cleaned,' he added with needless crudeness.

'Come on, let's get out of here,' Connor said after the Weasel had left with a smirk on his face. 'I'm getting claustrophobic.'

Connor ordered two lattes, only to be corrected by April, who wanted a skinny latte with skimmed milk. Connor looked his new co-worker up and down, from the blouse straining to contain her cleavage to the two-tone shoes. This old bird was certainly a character, he thought to himself.

Just as he was about to pay, April blew her healthy lifestyle cover by asking for a blueberry muffin, too. 'I'm bloody starving,' she explained. It had just gone 10 a.m.

Connor dispensed with the small talk and got down to the nitty gritty. 'So our new editor doesn't like crime stories?'

April said, 'That's strange, I heard it was human interest stories he didn't like. Well, that's explains a lot – like why we've been lumped together in a converted broom cupboard.'

They sat in silence, sipping their coffees and contemplating their situation.

'I'd rather they just paid me off,' moaned April.

'If newspapers can get out of paying you off they will. Gone are the days when they waved goodbye to you with a big fat cheque. What they do now is piss you off so much you leave. But where to? No one's hiring … well, not quite true, they're taking on kids for a third of our wages.'

'Hmmm, so what should we do? Get in touch with the union?' April said.

'The NUJ's toothless, bloody toothless,' said a frustrated Connor.

'Well, I've still got bills to pay,' added April needlessly.

A long period of silence followed.

'Well, I've never given up without a fight,' said Connor.

'Me neither,' said April, 'and I ain't about to go with a whimper.'

THE VIC

Selina Seth was discovered not far from her final sexual encounter. Her battered and broken body looked like it had been shaken to death, with each limb twisted at an unnatural angle. Her killer had made a decent attempt to conceal the corpse, but a dog walker discovered the grim scene before the businesswoman had even turned cold and immediately raised the alarm.

Although shocked by the gruesome sight, with the victim's hair matted to her head by blood and mud, there was still something vaguely familiar about her to the man taking his mutt for its morning constitutional. Later he had asked the detective who questioned him, 'Was she that jewellery lassie?'

Detective Chief Inspector David 'Bing' Crosbie surveyed the murder scene and sighed. He knew Selina's death would soon be common knowledge. He could feel the excitement in the air and hear the murmurings of the PCs manning the police line. Of course, Strathclyde had more than its fair share of murders, but this was different – this was a high-profile killing. It was certainly Crosbie's first 'celebrity' case in the twenty years since he had joined the force.

He swore repeatedly under his breath: 'Fuck, fuck, fuck, you stinking motherfucking turd.' Crosbie never cursed in front of fellow officers, but his inner monologue seemed to suffer from Tourette's Syndrome. It would often let rip over everything from police incompetence to politicians' meddling in police matters, or how it was a cast iron fact that his superior Detective Superintendent Cruickshank had only been promoted because he was a member of the same masonic lodge, golf club and gym as Chief Constable Ramsgate.

Whenever he was being addressed by Cruickshank – for his

superior only ever addressed, never consulted anyone beneath his rank – Crosbie's inner monologue would be doing cartwheels. 'If there was a Masters degree in brown-nosery, you'd pass with an A – that's A for dirty, back-stabbing arsehole' was the general theme for one of his inner barrages during which he maintained a silent, fixed grin.

But he wasn't smiling today. Selina Seth's death would be headline news, and with the press meant pressure, and pressure meant mistakes. He thought back to Jill Dando, the popular TV presenter shot dead on the doorstep of her London home in 1999. Amidst a media maelstrom, the police eventually did what they always do, and arrested the local loony – a man known to stalk females. In 2008 their suspect was acquitted after a retrial. Police had got the wrong man.

Crosbie did not intend to do the same. But that would be easier said than done with every newspaper and TV station in the country demanding answers, coming up with their own theories, all of which would be his job to investigate.

But first the victim.

Just as DCI Crosbie was pulling on his forensic suit and gloves to approach the crime scene, a call was made to a reporter on the *Daily Herald*. The dog walker had been severely warned by Crosbie's underling Detective Constable Marc Donohoe not to speak of his findings to anyone and had been reminded sternly that he would be found guilty of perverting the course of justice if he went bleating about it. This had not stopped Donohoe himself calling his friendly newspaper contact with the information, earning himself a handsome five hundred pound tip-off fee. Of course, it was illegal to pay a police officer under the Bribery Act, but newspapers had been carrying out the practice since time immemorial. And Connor Presley was only too happy to take the call from his contact. It meant the new Special Investigations desk had its first case.

THE DOOR KNOCK

The Seths lived in Dullatur on the outskirts of Glasgow. Although technically part of the sprawling new town of Cumbernauld, Dullatur had a distinctly old world feel to it, with many of the pale sandstone buildings dating back to the Victorian era. The Seths' home was down a bumpy single-track road called The Lane.

April loved property. Every Wednesday morning she always made a beeline for the *Daily Herald*'s property section. If she'd had her way she'd have been a writer for a homes and gardens magazine. 'What could be more fun than poking your nose around someone else's pad?' she'd say.

Many believe that the eyes are the windows to the soul, but April reckoned to really know someone you had to see how they lived and how they decorated their homestead. She pressed the buzzer on the gate's video intercom.

A croaky voice answered abruptly and asked what she wanted.

This was April's time to shine. She may have been past her prime but no one was better than this old hack on a doorstep. 'Is that Martin Seth?' she gushed. 'You probably won't remember me but we met at the *Daily Herald*'s model contest last year.' Truth be told, April had only seen the Seths from a distance sipping champagne with the previous editor Danny Brown at the city's Princes Square shopping complex, which the newspaper had hired for the annual event. As the paper's women's editor it was April's job to cover the beauty pageant and look after the contestants backstage, which mainly involved trying to stop them scratching each other's eyes out.

'Do you mind if I come in?' April asked hopefully. There was no answer but seconds later the two cast iron gates swung open.

The staff snapper Jack Kennedy had deliberately stayed out of sight of the video camera while April worked her magic. Now he slipped through the gates and fell into step behind her. There was no way he could go back to the office without a picture of the grieving widower.

April had always wanted to see the Seths' mansion and it didn't disappoint. A racing green Jaguar sat on the long gravel driveway. The front door to the large house was ajar. She chapped gently on the door and shouted through the crack, 'Can we come in?'

There was no answer, so she took that as a yes and let herself and the photographer into the hallway. A chessboard floor led to an extravagant marble staircase, above which a gaudy chandelier dangled. But April noticed that the place was in some disarray. It was beyond the normal family mess seen in most homes. Kids' clothes were dumped in piles, having not quite made it as far as the washing machine, and a slice of stale toast lay beside the hall phone. It wasn't just housework that had gone to pot, the place was suffering from long-term neglect. The scuffed walls were in desperate need of a lick of paint and several floor tiles were cracked.

April tentatively made her way to the rear of the house, shouting, 'Martin! Martin!' periodically.

There was still no answer. The rear of the old Victorian pile had a very contemporary glass and steel extension. April didn't think the mix of old and new worked, but she could see why the Seths had added it. One level down, the underwater lights of a swimming pool glittered.

She tried again. 'Martin! Martin!' Still no answer. April made her way towards the pool. Like the rest of the house it had seen better days; green slime clung to its sides and in the murky depths April could make out a dark shape. It was a body.

She screamed, 'Martin!' before quickly composing herself and turning to the photographer. 'You'll have to go in – I can't swim.'

Martin Seth coughed and spluttered as the full, and quite considerable, weight of April Lavender bore down on him.

Fortunately, she had remembered most of her first aid training from her days as a Navy Wren. April filled her lungs and engulfed Martin's mouth once more, blowing into his airways. Then she bumped his chest again, leaning down as hard as she could. But she wasn't the waif-like Wren she'd once been. Back then she'd had to kneel on the chest of the practice dummy to make the electric buzzer go off. This time the same manoeuvre had her subject gasping, 'Get off! You're killing me, you great, big fat lump.' So much for gratitude.

Martin Seth spat the remains of the slimy green pool from his lungs and slumped, dripping wet, against a sun lounger.

Having dived in to pluck Seth from the bottom of the pool the photographer was now busy capturing Martin's lowest moments on camera. His suicide attempt could be interpreted in two ways, either he was too griefstricken to carry on or he had done it because of a guilty conscience. That's the way the photographer saw it anyway. After years of peering down a camera lens almost everything became two-dimensional.

April fussed over Selina's widower. 'That was a very silly thing to do, Martin. What about your kids?'

Martin looked crestfallen.

'Right, cup of tea?' April suggested. She was of the belief that there was nothing that couldn't be cured with a cuppa. She wrapped a towel she found over one of the loungers and ushered him to the kitchen, carefully slipping in the first question: 'I'm so sorry for your loss, Martin. When were you told?'

'The cops called just after you rang the buzzer. They didn't say what was up exactly, but I knew it was Selina. I knew it had to be bad.'

April was many things, but she was nobody's fool. She knew a lie when she heard one.

Half an hour later the police did arrive – two CID detectives and two female family liaison officers. April filled them in with what had happened then was unceremoniously asked to leave as they conducted their inquiries. She called Elvis.

'What you got?' he answered without any preamble.

'A lying bastard,' replied April. 'And yourself?'

'An adulterous cow,' said Connor. 'Sounds like a match made in heaven. I'll call the Weasel.' He knew the first rule of journalism was to call the desk head immediately after a job. 'See you back at the broom cupboard,' he added.

THE CAT AND THE HAT

The Weasel could never actually admit that April and Connor had done well on their debut as the Special Investigations team, but he did announce to the news room when April returned, 'I told you to break the news to Martin – I didn't mean kill the cunt.' He knew he wasn't being factually accurate, but he never missed the opportunity to grandstand in front of his staff or use the c-word. In fact he said it so often in conference, fellow executives now called the daily meeting the Vagina Monologues.

Encouraged by the nervous smiles around him the Weasel turned to face April and Connor. 'Seth's death really was manna from heaven for you pair.'

He was right. With their guile, experience, contacts and a huge slice of luck, April and Connor were way ahead of the pack. By the time the next day's paper hit the streets, everyone in Scotland would be aware of Selina's death from the TV news bulletins. But the *Daily Herald* would have the added extra of Martin's suicide attempt, with the front-page splash: JEWELLERY QUEEN MURDERED: GRIEFSTRICKEN HUSBAND TRIES TO TAKE HIS OWN LIFE. And a strapline at the foot of the page boasting: SEE EXCLUSIVE PICTURES ON PAGES 2–9. Two by-lines would also share the front page: APRIL LAVENDER AND CONNOR PRESLEY, SPECIAL INVESTIGATIONS TEAM.

Connor and April had battered out their copy. He couldn't help but be impressed by the speed of the old burd. She had churned out every 'cough, spit and fart', as he described it, from Martin Seth and then added a timeline, from the estimated time of Selina's death to Martin's suicide bid. April Lavender was what was termed 'an operator' in the trade. She finished her copy, well before her young colleague, and playfully berated him. 'What's keeping you? I'm bloody starving.'

* * *

April was dog tired by the time she got home. The adrenaline of writing a front-page story had subsided and the day's events had left her exhausted. Constant tiredness due to her advancing years had become her biggest enemy. It made it harder to get up each day and face work, and it put her off attempting to lose weight.

Even trying to get her reluctant old cat Cheeka to go outside for a pee was a struggle. April stood with the front door ajar, trying to coax the moggy to move. After several words of encouragement the cat still hadn't budged an inch, so April gently pushed Cheeka with her foot, only to discover it was her black furry hat she'd been talking to. It had fallen on the floor from the coat stand behind the door.

Her eyesight was getting worse by the day. Maybe that's why she'd put on those odd shoes this morning. She felt as though she was falling apart at the seams, along with her career. Sure, she had mustered some fighting spirit today, but there would be other days when she'd have no stories or leads to work on. That's when the Weasel would be right on her case, making her feel like a failure or someone who was cheating the company out of a wage.

In the solitude of her bungalow in Glasgow's Southside, April suddenly felt very low. She had helped to pay for this place with the proceeds from her third divorce. Now the kids had gone along with hubby number three. Why were her relationships always doomed to fail?

Still, at least she had the cat for company. She poured a generous gin and tonic and went to sit in the armchair in front of the telly. As her ample behind lowered itself into the chair, April suddenly realised the place was occupied. She managed to catch herself just in time, spilling half her G&T in the process. After a quick glance April fumed, 'That bloody hat again,' and out of spite, plonked herself down firmly on top of it. The 'hat' let out a loud, anguished yowl. Cheeka had been fast asleep before being abruptly woken by the full weight of her owner's considerable behind.

While Connor was enjoying a beer in the Press Bar and April was vibrating a glass cabinet with her heavy snoring, DCI Crosbie was still working, poring over the statement from Selina's husband.

Like April, he too knew Martin was lying. Something wasn't right. Crosbie had stood back and observed Martin intently as he'd identified his wife's body in the morgue. Not a flicker of emotion, but by the time he had reached the front door where the media lay in wait, Martin had turned on the water works, tears streaming down his face conveniently for the cameras.

This was a man who one minute was trying to drown himself and the next perfectly capable of fulfilling his next-of-kin duties. He went from one extreme to the other – it was as if there were two Martins.

Crosbie hoped forensic results would shed more light on the case in the morning. Just as he was about to leave for home DS Cruickshank arrived unannounced. He looked harassed, taking his hat off and patting his thinning hair.

'This,' he said, deliberately taking his time, 'is a nightmare. Do we have anything yet, Crosbie? Anything at all?'

Nothing yet, you balding bastard, screamed Crosbie's suffering alter ego, *but as soon as I do, I'll make sure you take the credit, dickhead.*

'Nothing yet, sir,' Crosbie said out loud. 'A few discrepancies in the husband's statement that we'll check out, but forensics are due back in the morning.'

'Very well,' replied Cruickshank, 'but we need to get her murderer fast.'

'Oh, do you think so, moron?' Crosbie muttered.

'What was that, DCI Crosbie?'

The colour drained from Crosbie's face before he quickly composed himself. 'I think it'll be clearer in the morning.'

'Here's hoping, Inspector,' and with that the DS turned on his heels and left.

This Tourette's thing is getting worse, Crosbie thought to himself. It was bad enough cursing like a trooper in his head – he abhorred swearing – but now it was escaping into the real world he needed to seek help. Maybe he was cracking up? Maybe he'd seen the results of too much violence – Selina would be his forty-second murder case. He had a horrible feeling this case – and his condition – was going to get a lot worse before it got better.

COPYCAT KILLER

Osiris broke the whore's neck and dumped her body in a ditch just five miles down the M74 from where Selina had been killed at Strathclyde Park.

Every newspaper and TV channel had been plastered with details of her death. Osiris decided it was time to turn the country's morbid fascination with murder into blind panic now that a killer was on the loose.

That's why he had carried out a copycat killing. The prostitute he'd picked up in Glasgow's notorious Blythswood Square had clearly worked the streets for years and knew how to handle a violent punter, but no one she'd ever encountered had shown the same strength and ferocity as Osiris, who had broken her jaw with one punch and knocked her out with another, showing remarkable dexterity within the confines of the car.

Osiris hated coppers, and this would act as a distraction for what he had in mind. He knew time was short. Sooner or later the cops were going to get lucky and he wouldn't be able to bluff and bluster his way out of it. That simply could not be allowed to happen. Osiris had to be free to carry out his work, which, in his warped mind, he often considered charitable. Life couldn't have been so great for the whore he'd just dumped. As far as he was concerned it was a mercy killing. He was ridding the earth of another 'disease-spreading parasite' – no bad thing. But what he had planned next would be highly risky. He needed to concentrate. He needed his CDs.

Osiris pressed *play* on his car stereo and let the soothing words wash over him. 'People ask me, "How did you get to the top?" Then "How much do you earn?" usually follows.' Much laughter from the studio audience followed. The American voice continued. 'But only a loser asks questions like that. There is no quick fix or secret to get to the top. I had firm beliefs that what I was doing was right and different from all the rest. And I stuck to my guns.' Americans so loved speaking in clichés, but that bit still made Osiris smile. He too knew that what he was doing was right and different from the rest. The self-help guru added, 'As for how much I earned last year – it was two hundred million dollars when I floated my company, thank you very much.' That got whoops and rapturous applause from the studio crowd.

But Osiris cared little for cash. Killing was his currency.

FEELING PECKISH

April threw caution to the wind and ordered a full English breakfast in her favourite greasy spoon café. She felt ravenous this morning, stuffing whole bacon rashers wrapped in butter-sodden toast and dipped in the yolk of a fried egg into her mouth. Fifteen minutes later the huge chasm that had become her stomach was finally satisfied. She remembered a time when food wasn't the be all and end all of her life. In her late teens she had hardly eaten at all, much to the constant worry of her poor mother. 'Oh, Mum, I'm too busy to eat,' she'd say while getting dolled up for yet another night at the Zanzibar in Hope Street – Glasgow's premier hotspot at the time.

She gave a wry smile to herself and looked down at the mounds of flesh that now jutted out beyond her ample chest. 'What a little butterball I've become,' she muttered, once again too loudly.

The waitress Martel was used to the slightly batty old peroxide blonde speaking to herself. It didn't bother her as April always had a warm, ready smile and never failed to leave a tip. She poured April another cup of tea and placed a small pile of today's newspapers on the table beside her.

April smiled and said, 'Thanks, love,' before flicking through the pages. The *Daily Herald*'s main rival, the *Express*, had some dramatic headlines about Selina's death, but a quick scan through the copy confirmed they had nothing but the basic details – the jewellery queen was dead.

That wasn't the case in the *Daily Herald*, with the dramatic pictures of Martin Seth's body lying unconscious by the family pool.

April was pleased to see that, apart from the intro, most of her copy remained untouched. She didn't come from the school of writers who felt that every article they wrote was a potential

Pulitzer Prize winner and therefore should remain untouched by sub-editors – the plumbers of journalism. The 'subs' were the production journalists who actually made the reporters' articles fit into the spaces on the page. Many reporters had a them-and-us attitude to subs. There were, without doubt, good and bad ones – as there were good and bad reporters. The good subs would only change a reporter's copy to correct it or enhance it. A bad one would rewrite it for the sake of it, miss out the relevant points, change ages and sometimes even names. It was also not unknown that by the time they had rejigged the article, they had often forgotten who had written it, and occasionally even stuck someone else's by-line on it. But, as far as April was concerned, subs had bailed her out more often than dropped her in it, catching embarrassing spelling mistakes and, at worse, legals that would have had her before a judge on contempt of court. When she overheard reporters bitching about how a sub had rewritten their copy, April often wondered if they ever thanked them for repairing their spelling mistakes, appalling grammar or the horrendous legal gaffes that had slipped under the radar. Over time the subs knew April could put words together in roughly the right order and let her copy be.

She flicked through the rest of the paper, occasionally commenting on tales that caught her attention, blissfully unaware she was reading out loud. Ten minutes later she gathered her things and left a pound tip on the counter.

Martel said, 'You know, after you've talked us through the morning papers, there's no need for me to read them afterwards.'

April laughed. 'I really am a mad old, bat aren't I?'

Connor was slightly hungover. He sat slumped in his chair with a latte in hand and glanced up at April. She looked remarkably bright and breezy. He glanced at her feet. At least she was wearing the same coloured shoes today. That was a positive sign.

They hadn't even exchanged good-mornings before the Weasel kicked open the door to the broom cupboard. He didn't bother with any pleasantries. 'The editor wants to see you both in his office *now*.'

This meant official business. You never knew what to expect when summoned by the editor. Even Connor's favourite boss Danny Brown could make a career-changing decision on your behalf in a five-minute meeting in his office. Occasionally, it would be for a pat on the back – or herogram as they were called – but Connor remembered one piece of sound advice he'd been given by Badger: 'In this business one day you're a hero, the next a cunt.'

The pair were shown into Nigel Bent's office by his PA.

It was obvious Bent was a control freak, with a dash of OCD – everything on his oak-panelled desk was laid out in meticulous straight lines. Even the way he was sitting, with his two index fingers resting on his chin as if deep in thought, was stage-managed for the benefit of Connor and April.

Neither rated this editor, and not just because he'd been parachuted in by the company to replace the popular Danny Brown. There was something cold and dark about Bent. He was the sort of man who craved the title of editor and the power that came with it, rather than the job itself. The staff at the *Daily Herald* had rarely seen Bent since his appointment a month ago. He'd claimed in an introductory bulk email to staff that 'his door was always open', when in fact it was permanently shut.

Connor sensed that underneath the calm exterior, the sharp suits and the gelled strands of hair that did little to conceal Bent's baldness, there lurked a real bad bastard.

'Ah, April, Connor, good hit yesterday,' he said, sounding just a little too rehearsed. 'A very good hit.'

Maybe they'd been summoned for a herogram after all, but Bent was more of an email editor – why say something face to face when you can fire off a few emotionless words on a computer? There must be something else. And there was.

'But today I need to know if anyone knows why Selina was in that car park. Maybe ask your cop contacts, Connor? And, April, I want you to go back up to the Seths and see if Martin knew anything about her last movements. But go easy on Martin. He'll be raw and sensitive right now.'

Especially after April sat on his chest, Connor thought to himself.

*   *   *

Back in the broom cupboard April and Connor were silent. April
was the first to speak. 'Go easy on him? The entire country thinks
Martin did it and I'm told to go easy on him. Did you get the
impression Bent's worried about something?'

'Yup, he was way too friendly,' said Connor. 'The Weasel could
have told us to hit the cops and the doorstep. Bent's after something or at least needs to know something. Let's find out what he
really wants to know. Might be a good stick to beat him over the
head with.'

12

HEADLINE NEWS

The stereotypical image of a serial killer is one of some deranged loner sharpening his knives in front of a homemade altar in a blood-splattered basement surrounded by press clippings. But to be a successful serial killer requires a degree of social skills. He needs to blend in. How often when a mass murderer is caught do you hear a neighbour say on TV, 'He was such a quiet, normal chap, too.'

No one who saw Osiris having a pint in the Lab bar in Glasgow city centre that lunchtime would have suspected that a deranged psychopath lurked within.

'Another pint, Vinnie?' said the tubby regional manager Chick McAulay.

'Don't mind if I do,' he replied cheerfully.

'What d'you make of this rich bitch, Vinnie?' MacAulay waved the front page of the *Daily Herald* at him and continued. 'Came from fuck all but suddenly thought her shite smelled better than the rest of us because she was *friend to the stars*.' He flicked to April's spread and pointed at the pictures of Martin Seth at his lowest ebb, having just been dragged from the bottom of a swimming pool. 'There's your murderer. That's why he tried to top himself. Guilty. Guilty as hell. Case closed.' Having wrapped up the Seth mystery, MacAulay moved effortlessly onto the football.

If only life were that easy for DCI Crosbie. He had read Martin Seth's statement four times since arriving at his desk at 7 a.m. He then turned his attention to April's interview with Seth in the *Daily Herald*. He liked newspapers, particularly the *Herald*, and had once nurtured ambitions to be a reporter, but try as he might he couldn't make the breakthrough. A young family soon demanded a steady income rather than the bits and bobs of freelance work he brought in. And so he joined the Strathclyde Police where he rose steadily through the ranks from flat foot to Detective Chief Inspector. He knew colleagues who had attained higher ranks and wished they hadn't. Their career choice meant a full-time desk job and constant computer work. They no longer got to chase the bad guys or even use their powers of arrest. *What's the point in being a cop if you never nick some cunting lowlife fuck?*

Crosbie remained quiet for a moment, scanning the room for reaction to his outburst. Thankfully, it appeared to have gone unspoken. That reminded him. He had an appointment with a shrink at three. He'd gone private because even though the force offered free counselling and psychological services he didn't trust the claims they were confidential. Somewhere they'd have to log his problem, and if the top brass wanted to get their hands on it they could. And that would mean anything said could be taken down and used against you.

Crosbie reckoned he'd have enough time to bring Martin Seth in for questioning and make his three o'clock session with the psychiatrist. It was an appointment he didn't have a hope in hell of making.

Martin was also flicking through the newspapers Selina had insisted were delivered each morning so she could scour for the next celebrity to front a new product range. Of course, she could only really afford the stars who were on the slide, and not the ones who were hot to trot and would make ridiculous financial demands. He thought how ironic it was that his wife would have loved the publicity her sudden and violent death had caused. Not only was she the main splash story on every Scottish daily newspaper, she had also earned front-page coverage on the bigger-selling, London-based papers.

It helped that Selina had been, technically speaking, a star in her own right, thanks to countless daytime TV appearances and her recent film debut in a low-budget British film *The Only Way Is Up*. The film's makers claimed it was chock-a-block with the country's 'most exciting new stars' – code for a cast of nobodies and minor Z-listers, the famous-for-being-famous type.

Selina played a 'sexy ice queen from Antarctica' in a fantasy dream sequence, which turned out to be as awful as it sounds. It was shot inside a giant freezer in an abattoir in London's east end, so the producers wouldn't need to spend any of their dwindling funds on 'South Pole' special effects.

Selina had been included at the eleventh hour after a silicone-enhanced starlet from a reality show, the original choice for the role, had mistakenly feared her breast implants would freeze solid, telling the stunned producer, 'I ain't freezing my tits off after paying ten grand for these beauties.'

But Selina had excelled on screen. As far as she was concerned she had been acting for all of her life, pretending to be something she was not. She could also see the endless publicity opportunities as businesswoman *turned actress*. Selina gave countless interviews before the film was even released, ramping up her role and the drama, claiming she had at one point 'gone hypothermic' in the giant freezer and even boldly stating that she had suffered frost-bite, despite the lack of evidence.

What she had omitted was the fact that she had paid £15,000 for her role, after answering a plea for funds from the film's producer, who claimed they would not be able to release their production without a final five-figure cash injection. Fearing her debut movie part was about to be canned and the humiliation that would ensue after bragging so publicly about her 'starring role', she once again begged her husband to loosen the company purse strings. He eventually agreed in the hope of a quiet life.

As a reward for helping to save his appalling film, the producer even shared his supply of dope with a grateful Selina. She spent the three-day shoot getting high, hot and horny with the producer in his trailer. Then at the wrap party in London, Selina was captured by the paparazzi stumbling out of a nightclub hanging on to the arm of one of her hunky fellow co-stars, much to the annoyance of her producer-lover. She'd been so wasted she barely remembered having sex with the young actor, and the following day their 'affair' had hit all the tabloids. It helped that Selina was married and had therefore been unfaithful, but the fact that the young hunk's semi-permanent girlfriend was the surgically enhanced reality star Selina had replaced in the film gave the story extra spice.

A few days later Selina had taken great delight instructing the company's law firm Mallicks & Co. to issue a statement to the media: 'It is with great regret that after eighteen years of marriage Selina and Martin Seth are to separate. The split is amicable ... there is no one else involved ... they will continue as active directors in Seth International, the company they co-founded and now the country's largest online jewellery firm, endorsed by celebrities including Dannii Minogue.'

Martin had laughed at the absurdity of the 'amicable split' reference. 'How can any split be amicable? Do you just casually mention over dinner one night, 'Oh, that was a lovely lasagne, dear, and by the way I'm off, and I want half of everything,' he had bitched to a friend. He had actually welcomed the split, as it was a break from the mental turmoil. Selina had in fact manufactured the whole separation to put their flagging jewellery business back in the news. Well, that's what she claimed, but Martin knew her motives were far more self-serving than that. How he had loathed her as she sat in the study of the house they could ill afford, which Martin believed perfectly summed up their marriage as 'all facade', and waited for the texts and emails of condolences to flood in. He remembered thinking Selina had had some sort of seizure when she screamed and leapt from her chair, brandishing her BlackBerry at head height and shouting, 'Dannii's texted! Dannii Minogue texted!' Even though they had paid the antipodean talent show judge half a million quid, she rarely texted Selina.

'Oh, this split is the best thing ever,' Selina had beamed. 'We should have separated years ago,' she added, embracing her weary husband. Martin remembered how he had held her tightly and for a brief moment saw a look of genuine warmth and affection in his wife's eyes that he hadn't seen in years. Sadly, the moment had been fleeting and Selina quickly wriggled free before heading to their bedroom. For one glorious moment Martin had thought his wife was going to offer to make love to him, something she hadn't done either sober, or without being in the arms of another man hours earlier, for as long as he could remember. Instead she had grabbed a suitcase from the top shelf of their walk-in wardrobe and barked, 'Pack. There will be photographers

arriving outside soon and we need to give them what they want.'
Then with her habitual change of mind, she added, 'No, wait a
minute. I'll get more sympathy if I leave.'

She hastily set about stuffing clothes and underwear into her case,
not forgetting the wraps of her favourite drug of choice, crysta meth,
which she had become so reliant on. Towards the end of her life
Selina had made little attempt to cover up her drug use. She'd once
been stopped for speeding in her car with flecks of white powder
caked around her nostrils. The police officers had inexplicably turned
a blind eye after Selina had worked her charm on them, giving them
free jewellery from a bag of new stock samples in her boot and promising the officers they would get lucky with their wives that night.
One of the cops had cheekily replied, 'I'd rather get lucky with you,'
which he did, two nights later in the back of her Jaguar in a deserted
Lidl car park. Sure, Martin had tried drugs a few times himself, but
he'd been in his early twenties. Why Selina, who was now forty, felt
she needed to snort the stuf daily was beyond him. She was a middle-
aged mum of two, but in her head she was a rising celebrity who
craved the limelight. Selina had picked up her case in one hand and
slipped the other around Martin's waist, pulling him close to peck
his cheek. She'd smiled. 'Don't worry, we won't be separated for long.
We'll announce we're getting back together in a few months' time –
think of all the magazine interviews I can do on the back of it.'

Martin remembered her checking her make-up before she left,
ready for the press photographers who were waiting outside her
front gate. She'd planned to drive slowly past them with her window
down to make sure they got their shot. He'd watched as his wife
suddenly turned and began waving at him. He waved back before
he realised it was her BlackBerry she was excitedly flapping around.

'Amanda Holden!' she'd shrieked, 'Amanda Holden has just texted
to say how sad she is to hear we've separated. She must have got my
number from Dannii. I can't believe it, Amanda fucking Holden.'

He'd laughed wryly at the expletive Selina had accidentally let
slip, which she had tried so hard to eradicate from her vocabulary,
and thought, 'You can take Selina Seth out of Glasgow, but you'll
never take Glasgow out of Selina Seth.'

*   *   *

April trudged down the same gravel path Martin was currently staring at, lost in his reminiscences. She was alone this time. Having been stung the day before when the *Daily Herald* photographer captured his attempt at a watery grave, Martin had told April via the video intercom at the main gates to leave the snapper behind this time.

He was waiting for her outside the main door. He looked in a terrible state with his tousled bed hair, dishevelled clothes, which he'd clearly slept in, and a stubble so dark it looked blue. He rubbed the sleep from his eyes, sat down on the front step and turned his face up to the warmth of the early morning sunshine. Before April could speak he said, 'I better appreciate the daylight while I still can – they think I killed her.'

'Did you kill her, Martin?' April asked gently.

'No,' he spluttered, 'I did not.' He paused for a moment as if he wanted to add something else, but then thought better of it.

April's Dictaphone, which she'd placed at the top of her handbag between them, had recorded every word while Jack Kennedy's telescopic lens snapped frame after frame of the would-be murder suspect and April together. The pictures would have been actionable as Martin was on his private property, however, Kennedy had made a point of taking them from the public road, albeit he'd had to hack some undergrowth to get a clear shot. His job was done and that was the main thing. Scribblers, as the snappers called the reporters, could always pick up a phone to ask questions they'd forgotten. Photographers didn't have that luxury.

Kennedy heard vehicles approaching and quickly returned to his car, his face a perfect picture of innocence. 'Rozzers,' thought Kennedy, 'they've come to take him away – this will make a perfect shot.'

The electronic gates swung open to let the two unmarked CID cars through, and Kennedy quickly took up his position again by the edge of the road. It'd be the second day in a row the snapper would capture Martin Seth at the worst points in his life. As the handcuffs were snapped around Martin's wrists Kennedy muttered, 'Poor sod,' as his shutter repeatedly clicked.

13

THE SECOND VIC

While Martin Seth was being taken into custody, Crosbie was speeding towards another crime scene. The body of a middle-aged female had been found in deep undergrowth near the New Lanark turn-off on the M74. Crucially, it was within a five-mile radius of the Seth murder scene. Crosbie hoped and prayed they weren't connected.

A motherfucking serial cunting killer, his inner monologue screamed out, *that's all I horse cocking need.*

The blue lights flashed and the siren blared from the top of his police car, but inside Crosbie sighed. He really needed a holiday. He'd just turned forty, which had made him acutely aware that there was less life in front of him as there was behind him, and he was also well aware that the average age a police officer survived after retirement was a measly five years. If Crosbie got out at the earliest opportunity, at forty-eight, that would give him just thirteen more years of life.

The cunting trick then, fanny face, is not to retire then.

Oh great. His alter ego had now taken to insulting him. At this rate he'd be lucky to make it to forty-one in the force before he had a full nervous breakdown. Was it any wonder, really? He was just about to witness his forty-third murder victim and yet again have reaffirmed that humans can indeed do the most awful things to one another.

There was a nip in the air as Crosbie stepped out into the September sunshine. Forensics gave him their initial report, which was pretty much what he knew already, with one added fact: the victim's neck had been broken. Crosbie let out a heavy sigh. Even his inner monologue had the good sense to stay quiet. The detective knew the press would immediately link the two murders before forensics had had a chance to even get their samples off to the laboratory, and would splash that a violent serial killer was on the loose. He hated the term 'serial killer' as it made his life a whole lot harder. Apart from the public hysteria, which would be whipped up into a frenzy by the media, he believed it would cloud the investigating team's judgment. They would look for links that weren't there.

The same thing had happened in Glasgow in the 1960s, when three women who had been to the city's popular Barrowland Ballroom had been strangled. The killer had been dubbed Bible John by the press because a tall, fair-haired, bible quoting man had allegedly been witnessed leaving the nightspot with one of the victims.

Bible John was never caught. For a year and a half – from his first victim to his third – the city had been gripped by fear. Then suddenly he stopped. Rumours circulated of Bible John's true identity, from a criminal who'd been jailed for another crime to a rogue policeman and a cover up by the force.

Crosbie, too young to remember the case, always believed his colleagues of old had simply botched the original investigation. He'd spent hours going through the case files – with the murders unsolved they were still active – and could almost feel the hysteria screaming from the formal reports. Everyone working that case was looking for a serial killer.

Of course, the original investigation team didn't have the benefit of DNA evidence, but the modern police force did, and in 1998 they exhumed the body of a prime suspect. At the time Crosbie was new to CID but even as a rookie detective he suspected this was an unwise move from a glory-seeking top brass, and unfortunately he was proved right. The DNA from the dead murder suspect did not match the evidence left at the scene of the crime. Crosbie believed that the mysterious Bible John had killed just one, perhaps two, of the three unfortunate girls whose night on the tiles ended in violence.

And he certainly didn't believe that the same hands which had killed Selina Seth had killed the battered prostitute in front of him. By the positioning of her limbs, twisted into the same shape as Selina's corpse, someone clearly wanted him to believe that, but this copycat killer must have seen Selina's last moments as the crime scene picture of her body had never been released. He now needed to catch two killers.

Martin Seth was calmness personified as he sat by himself in Maryhill nick, sipping coffee from a plastic cup and flicking through a copy of *Metro*. It was an old one – no mention of his dead wife. He looked at the date at the top of the page: 5 September. That was just three days ago. Before his world had been turned upside down. Before Selina's death. Before he'd become a prime suspect. He'd like to think that on 5 September life had been comparatively normal, but that wasn't true.

Being married to Selina these past few years could never have been described as normal. She hadn't bothered covering up her affairs or, to be more accurate, her one night stands. Arriving home at dawn, drunk, underwear in her handbag, had almost become the norm. Martin had even learned to accept it. With his self-esteem at rock bottom he hadn't even felt humiliated any more. It was trying the keep the business afloat that had really taken its toll.

A picture in his study at home showed him posing with his five-a-side football side. He looked at least ten years younger. But the photograph had been taken less than two years ago. Now his hair and skin were greying, his face heavily lined from worry and a permanent frown. He no longer played football, he just didn't have the energy, and his sex drive was in his boots, which might have explained why his wife played away.

Every waking minute of every day was spent with his head in the company's books. They were actually making money thanks to Martin's hard work, but jewellery is an expensive game with a lot of overheads. Cash flow was the main problem. The retailers would take an age to pay and gold traders don't take IOUs.

Then there was Selina. The businesswoman who lived like a pop star. Although she was barred from making the company's most crucial decisions on her own, she was still the face of Seth International and refused point blank to rein in her spending. She'd taunt Martin during their many furious rows that he was 'just an accountant' and she was the 'creative one' in the partnership. She did have a point. And it was also true that she had to entertain department store head buyers, but Selina's 'entertaining' usually moved quickly from bottles of Bollinger to the bedroom.

Lately, she'd spent a lot of time romancing a big player at Tesco. Her credit card bills for expensive London restaurants and hotels had been mind-boggling, but Martin knew only too well that the account could have been the answers to their prayers.

It'd been close, too, before she died.

DCI Crosbie entered the room having come straight from his second murder scene in two days. He sat down wearily and looked at the widower and his female lawyer. Crosbie was the first to speak. 'Hello, Martin, I'm Detective Chief Inspector Crosbie, but if you're a good lad, you can call me Bing. Now listen, I'm very tired, and I can't be arsed trying to coax information out of you. You're an intelligent man, so how about you just tell me the truth and nothing but the truth?'

14

THE SUSPECTS

April and Connor had agreed to go for a coffee in Starbucks after they'd finished filing their copy. As Martin Seth had been arrested, April's interview could not be used as it was sub judice. Events had overtaken her exclusive chat with murder suspect number one, anyway, after the discovery of Jackie McIvor, a well-known street worker whose neck had been broken and her body dumped in a ditch.

Connor had been sent to the crime scene where yet again his friendly copper on police line duties had managed to slip him a few more nuggets of information that would keep the *Daily Herald* ahead of the pack.

April and Connor had left the office as the splash was being designed on screen – WOMAN NO. 2 MURDERED, SETH'S HUSBAND ARRESTED. It was certainly striking, but both felt uneasy about it.

'I don't think Martin could kill anyone, never mind two women in two days,' April said, emptying her fourth sugar sachet into her latte and taking a bite out of her Danish pastry.

Connor looked at the empty sachets with disdain. 'Do you know what? I don't think I've met anyone who eats as much as you do.'

April let out a raucous laugh. 'I know – wherever do I put it all?' She patted her wide hips.

They were silent for a moment, stirring their coffees absent-mindedly.

Connor was the first to speak. 'Well, I've never met him, but it'd take a special kind of psychopath to kill twice in two days – it's almost unheard of.'

'He honestly doesn't have it in him. He looks fairly fit but he's not strong enough to have snapped someone's neck,' April mused.

'Don't be so sure. Look at Peter Tobin, a right wee insignificant guy, yet the brutality he inflicted on his victims was horrific.'

Tobin was a small, wiry man who had kept his emotions in check throughout his police interviews and the search for three separate murder victims. The facade had only slipped once when he was being led from the High Court in Glasgow to a prison van where he'd kicked a kneeling *Daily Herald* photographer Paul Kielty in the neck. Before the snapper had passed out, he'd managed to fire off one frame of Tobin's evil face twisted and contorted with rage – so obviously the real Tobin his poor victims had seen before he sadistically took their lives.

'I still can't believe Paul Kielty didn't win a press award for that picture,' spat Connor. 'And who did they give it to? Some twat who'd taken a picture of a Highland cow in the snow. That sums up this bloody industry. Do you know what the biggest problem is with newspapers today? Tyrants. There aren't enough tyrants who want to be proprietors any more. It's all shareholders wanting their slice of the profits now. But newspapers are about gut instinct – not playing the market.'

'And what,' interrupted April, 'does that have to do with Selina and Martin?'

'Well, they're in the fashion business. Again, something you need to have a feel for. That needs a tyrant at the top, too. So who was the tyrant of the duo – Martin? I don't think so. It was Selina. Tyrants make great captains of industry but they also make great enemies. Find Selina's enemies and we'll find who snapped her neck.'

April sighed. 'But where do we begin? I remember a wee lassie from Selina's office came to see me a few years back. Charelle or Chantal or something?'

'Chantal Cameron. She was the office dog's body. Like Selina's shadow for a while. Went everywhere with her,' Connor replied.

'That's the one. Selina fired her and she came into see me bumping her gums, hinting at all sorts. But she wanted £10,000 up front to tell her story and the same again on publication.

'Well, we weren't going to pay that sort of money. I managed to haggle her down to a grand. Then she changed her mind and that was the end of that.

'But Chantal was just one of several. Selina's sacked so many staff she needed to fit a revolving door. They'll all be bearing grudges.' April reckoned.

"Nah, too obvious. The ones who were still working for her bear even bigger grudges. She was a total nightmare. But they're all women and there's no way a woman killed Selina.

'Maybe there's someone who sees himself as Selina's equal but who's been crossed by her. A previous lover? Although I don't think even the *Daily Herald* has enough resources to track them all down. You should trawl through cutts, mainly the business papers, and see if there were any lawsuits against Seth International that may have slipped under the radar.'

'Oh no,' screeched April, 'you know I'm useless with Factiva.' Factiva was the new online newspaper archive system – known as 'cutts' – that had replaced the old Telnet system which had been in place for fifteen years. 'The bastards only went and changed Telnet just as I'd learned to master it,' she added with no hint of a joke.

Connor laughed. 'They can upgrade the system but they can't upgrade our April Lavender.'

Apart from establishing a timeline of Martin Seth's movements on the day of his wife's murder, the formal interview had been unproductive. Crosbie had asked him directly if he'd killed his wife. Martin had replied with a firm 'No' before his lawyer had intervened. He was still a suspect, but as this was such a high-profile active case, Crosbie would have to pursue all other lines of inquiry.

Crosbie was thinking along the same lines as Connor. He reckoned that Selina Seth's sacked office junior was unlikely to have been involved in murder, but he still had to send a couple of detectives to interview the former staff member about her whereabouts when her ex-boss was brutally killed. Crosbie knew it would be a dead end.

He also wanted to find another disgruntled business associate with a major grudge. He could take his pick. Then there was the second case of the murdered prostitute Jackie McIvor, which

Crosbie was determined to keep separate from the Selina investigation. The man who'd killed Jackie was likely to be a known user of street workers. He'd most likely have previous for assault and possibly had killed before.

Crosbie hoped that by morning forensics would confirm that he was indeed after two different murders, even if the newspapers were determined there was only one. He afforded himself a wry smile. 'Print and be cunting damned. I wish my life was so pissing easy.' That reminded him, he needed to see his psychiatrist sooner rather than later.

April was one step ahead of DCI Crosbie and his team.

She was sitting in a Starbucks having an 8 a.m. meeting with Selina's former employee. Chantal Cameron had threatened to spill the beans on her time working for Selina, before she had suddenly clamed up. No cheque she'd subsequently been offered from a string of April's tabloid rivals to reveal all about her rich and famous employer could break her silence.

But now Selina was dead, Chantal had agreed to meet April once more. The reporter had ordered two lattes and the pair sat outside so they could smoke. Chantal was in the mood to get a lot off her fake chest. It transpired that she had been more than just Selina's dog's body. She'd also procured illegal drugs for her.

Chantal explained: 'I used to talk to Selina when I brought her coffee in the morning. We got quite close. She was like a big sister to me.

'Then one day she said she was feeling really down and tired and asked if I could think of anything to help her out.

'I'd do a bit of speed and the likes out clubbing at the weekends and actually had some on me. She said she'd never tried drugs before but was well up for it. She paid me out of petty cash. Then the next day she asked me for some more.

'Within a few weeks I was running errands left, right and centre on so-called company business, when all I was doing was picking up stuff from my dealer. She was into everything. Speed. MDMA. Blues, you name it.

'The speed was to get her hyped up before meetings, diazepam to bring her back down again. She also liked a bit of hash to get her off to sleep. She even asked me to get her crystal meth once.

'But then she sacked me.'

'Why?' April asked.

"Cos I was doing a bit of skimming,' Chantal replied nonchalantly.

'Skimming?' April enquired.

'I could skim around five hundred pounds a week for myself, plus what I needed for personal use,' Chantal replied, before deciding she needed to justify her stealing, 'but you have to remember it was my neck on the line. If I'd been busted then I would have taken the full rap – Selina had made that very clear. She was paranoid about being caught. But then paranoia and drugs kind of go hand in hand.'

'Who was your dealer?' April asked.

'I'm not at liberty to say,' Chantal replied coolly, 'but he's into drugs in a big way and not the sort you cross.'

'How much was Selina spending on drugs every week?' April asked.

'By the end? Up to two grand,' Chantal replied from behind her oversized shades.

'How much was your salary?' April asked.

'I was on buttons as a junior - twelve grand a year,' Chantal snorted.

'But you were earning another twenty-five on the side tax-free. You're quite the little entrepreneur,' April said.

'Look, I didn't come here for you to look down your nose at me. That bitch fired me after all the risks I took on her behalf. So what if she discovered I was ripping her off? What she was doing was illegal, too. I told her I'd expose her drug habit if she didn't pay me off.'

'Is that what happened. Did Selina buy your silence?' April asked.

'Er, no. I ended up getting another job,' Chantal added shiftily.

April knew she was lying. But as far as she was concerned Chantal was a symbol of everything that was wrong with today's generation: all me, me, me. Drugs and extortion came so easily to Chantal. It was just another bargaining tool. She was clearly a girl with issues and a massive chip on her shoulder. When April had been in her mid-twenties she would have been delighted to be worked for a rich and famous company boss. But that didn't appear to be enough any more. Chantal wanted to live the high life, too, having done nothing to deserve it.

April picked up the bill, thanked Chantal for her time and left with the excuse that she had another meeting to go to. Really, she was desperate to head to her favourite café, the Peccadillo.

Fifteen minutes later she took her usual seat. She was particularly hungry this morning. Dipping her link sausage into the yolk of her fried egg April muttered out loud, 'I blame X Factor and Pop Idol and all these talent shows. Kids just want to turn up and be famous now. They don't want to do the years of hard graft to get there.'

The waitresses and the regulars were used to April airing her thoughts in public, but she drew some looks from those who didn't know her.

'Mind if I join in your conversation?' Connor beamed.

'Oh,' April laughed, 'was I talking to myself again? I better stop that. People might think I'm mad.'

'There's no "might" about it, my batty old friend. Right, what have you got?'

April recounted her meeting with Chantal Cameron. At the end Connor had just one question: 'How did Selina know Chantal was ripping her off unless someone told her? I'm guessing it was the dealer and I have a funny feeling I know who it is.'

15

ANCHORED DOWN

'Oh, look what the cat dragged in,' roared Badger to a packed Anchorage bar in Yoker's Kelso Street.

Connor could see that his old mentor was three sheets to the wind, which meant he'd shifted a colossal amount of booze. Badger was rarely drunk – more like constantly 'topped up', as Connor used to say.

The young mentee – as he used to jokingly be called – was greeted with a bear hug from his old mentor and proudly introduced to the Anchorage regulars.

Connor then steered his old friend to a quieter corner. 'I need to meet the detective in charge of the Seth case. Crosbie. Known as Bing. Doesn't frequent any boozers as far as I'm told.'

'Crosbie, Crosbie,' pondered Badger, 'I've never heard of him. I'll sort something out for you. Anyway, how are things back at the ranch? Still hanging in there by your fingertips, I see. Has that cunt Bent no' been found out yet?'

'You're just bitter because he sacked you,' Connor teased.

Badger pinched Connor's cheek hard in something that passed for affection before announcing, 'I'm off for a pish,' and staggering off towards the toilet.

One of Badger's booze buddies Wee Al approached Connor. Wee Al was around six feet four with a ruddy drinker's complexion like Badger's. He plonked himself down on the seat next to Connor and sighed, 'He's ill, you know.'

Connor brushed it off. 'No wonder with the amount he drinks.'

'No, he's really ill,' Wee Al added, touching Connor's hand to emphasise the point. 'He speaks of you all the time. You're like the son he never had.'

Badger and his wife Rita had never had children. He'd never explained why.

Wee Al continued, 'He thinks the world of you. He's always banging on about "Elvis this" and "Elvis that". But he's dying … that's why he's drinking more than ever. He's in pain.'

Connor felt a wave of emotion crash over him. He'd never had a dad growing up and Badger had become something of a father figure.

Badger returned singing 'Blue Suede Shoes'. 'Come on, Elvis, geez a wee shake of those snake hips,' he demanded.

Connor needed to speak to him in the cold light of day. He'd take his opportunity tomorrow, hopefully, when Badger called with details on how to meet Crosbie.

Osiris was seriously hacked off. He'd spent the day travelling from one faceless industrial unit to another for a day of meetings with various depot managers. Because he was from head office he got nothing but moans from the branch bosses about how they'd run things differently. Osiris would put on his best sympathetic expression but inwardly he was glad these morons were basically nothing more than over-promoted truck drivers.

But that wasn't the reason Osiris was annoyed. The prostitute he'd killed had made all the front pages in Scotland and was linked with the death of that rich bitch, Selina Seth, but the detective in charge of the investigation had been at pains on the lunchtime news to keep both murder investigations separate.

DCI Crosbie's stern face filled the plasma screen in Edinburgh's Burke and Hare pub where Osiris was having a lunchtime pint with yet another transport manager. He found this branch head particularly tedious as he was a clubhouse bore, full of golf jokes – all of which Osiris had heard before.

'At this moment in time we are not connecting the deaths of Mrs Seth and Jacqueline McIvor. We'll obviously keep an open mind, but I'd like to assure the public that we do not believe this is the work of a serial killer and I'd like to ask the country's media to show responsibility and restraint in their reporting of these separate cases.'

Crosbie hated appearing on television. He wasn't like Detective Superintendent Cruickshank who loved the sound of his own voice and his looks even more. He'd taken a calculated risk making such a bold statement. Surprisingly, it wasn't the murderers he was most wary of, it was the press. By having a dig at them in public, basically rubbishing all of today's front pages, he could expect a huge backlash – especially if one of the killers struck again. He was gambling on having flushed them out by then.

Osiris watched intently as Crosbie made his announcement on the TV news. He began to hatch a plan that would take him way out of his comfort zone. But it was a risk he believed was worth taking.

April Lavender was eating again. 'Relentless grazing', as Connor called it, but she simply couldn't help herself. She felt hungry every couple of hours. And not just hungry – 'positively starving' as she was fond of saying.

She'd long given up on the bathroom scales, which were now covered in dust after being kicked, unloved, under the U-bend, but she did fancy enrolling in swimming classes at her local pool. Although she'd once been a Wren she'd never learned to swim. The last time she'd been to the 'baths', as they were called in Glasgow, to thrash around was when she was ten.

Her dad had bought her the biggest bag of chips afterwards, smothered in salt and vinegar. Lovely. She could still taste them. 'Oh bugger, now I'm desperate for a bag of chips.' After getting the daily dose of self-loathing out the way, April felt a lot better after polishing off a full Scottish breakfast, which is much like an English breakfast, except with a uniquely Scottish potato scone – a triangle of baked flour and potato, lightly fried and possessing the ability to soak up other food's saturated fats like a sponge.

April had decided on a different diet strategy, opting for a hearty breakfast – instead of her two rolls and bacon – followed by a moderate lunch, then a hearty dinner. She hoped this would diminish her desire for snacks. She smiled at the waitress Martel and said, 'There's method in my madness, you see.'

As usual, the waitress in the Peccadillo didn't have the foggiest idea what April was wittering on about but decided to humour her, 'Well, I hope it works out for you.'

April gave her a knowing wink. 'And if it fails, well, it'll just be our little secret.'

The waitress turned on her heels and brushed by Connor who had just come in.

He took one look at the girl's bemused face and said to April, 'That poor girl looks completely baffled – what pish have you been spouting this morning?'

April rarely took offence, which was just as well as she had to put up with plenty of insults. Instead she gave her trademark dirty laugh, left the correct change and headed for the door.

On the way out Connor tugged the waitress's sleeve and whispered, 'You're lucky, you just have to listen to her in the morning – I have to put up with her insanity all day.'

This waitress smiled then blushed. Connor was more attractive and better mannered than her usual clientele.

He easily read her body language, feeling a small stirring in his loins, and thought to himself, 'It's been a while.'

Someone else picked up on the vibes, too. 'Keep it in your pants, you dirty boy,' April said as they made their way to the office.

Connor made a mental note to himself. April was definitely a lot more perceptive than she let on.

Badger was Connor's first call of the day. His old mentor repeatedly had to cover his mouthpiece as he exploded into hacking coughing fits.

'You need to get that checked out,' Connor said tentatively, already anticipating the abusive answer.

'What are you? My doctor or my wife?' Badger growled, 'And anyway I have checked it out. I'm getting the test results at the end of the week. But enough of that bollocks. Your man Crosbie is a runner, mad for it apparently. Never could understand that myself – pound, pound, pound, bore, bore, bore. He's running the Glasgow half-marathon from George Square on Sunday. He's in the blue group, whatever that is. Something to do with the expected finishing time.' Connor could hear the flicking of pages while Badger checked his notepad. 'Crosbie runs it in about one hour thirty-five,' he added. 'Better get those shorts on, Elvis, and you'll need to swap the blue suede shoes for proper trainers.'

'Oh crap, I haven't run in years. How long is a half-marathon again?' The anxiety in Connor's voice was clearly audible.

Badger laughed loudly before succumbing to another coughing fit. He eventually managed to croak, 'Thirteen miles. But it's your only chance to meet him. He does bugger all else except work and run. Oh, and someone wants to meet you today. Very important. Be at the Portman bar at noon.'

'You know it's hard to get any time out of the sausage factory these days. Who is it?'

Badger gave a one-word reply: 'Harris.'

'Colin Harris – now what the hell did he want?' Connor thought to himself.

Back in the broom cupboard he told April about his rendez-vous with one of Glasgow's most lethal gangland enforcers turned author and alleged legitimate businessman. Now it was Connor's turn to speak his thoughts out loud. 'Legitimate, my arse.' He turned accusingly to April. 'Your insanity is rubbing off.'

The Weasel interrupted their conversation with his usual absence of pleasantries. 'The editor wants to see you both in his office now.'

Bent was sitting in his usual well-rehearsed pose behind his large mahogany desk, chin resting on his index fingers as if deep in thought. He didn't even make eye contact when April and Connor were shown in by his PA, launching into a question instead: 'Any news?'

Both reporters detected the hint of anxiety in the editor's voice, and both decided to toy with him.

'Well, I'm trying for an address for Jackie McIvor's mum,' April said.

Bent snapped 'No, not with the scumbag prostitute. Are the police getting anywhere with the Seth killer? What's this Crosbie character got to say off the record?'

'I don't know,' apologised Connor, knowing full well those were three words all editors hated, 'but I'm hoping to meet him this weekend.'

Bent was silent.

April's curiosity got the better of her. 'You seem very concerned about this case – did you know Selina well?'

A look of outrage swept across Bent's face, and April butted in before he could speak, 'I think everyone's been shocked by her death. They will find her killer.'

Bent slumped back in his chair, and eventually mumbled, 'You're right, we are all shocked. I had lunch with her the day before she was murdered. I just want the bastard caught.'

'So you don't think it was her husband then?' enquired Connor.

'No, I don't. Too obvious,' Bent said.

Funny how an editor's real views often betrayed what they put in their papers. 'Well, I shall hopefully find out Crosbie's real views, too,' Connor added.

Bent didn't answer as he stared unfocused at some imaginary spot on the carpet.

Connor and April took the silence as their cue and quietly slipped out his office leaving Bent to his thoughts.

'He certainly knows more than he's letting on,' April remarked.

16

COLIN 'THE HITMAN' HARRIS

The Portman bar was unimaginatively named after Portman Street where it sat on a corner in Glasgow's rundown Kinning Park district. Like many of the pubs in the area it had thrived when heavy industry ruled. But those days were long gone. Now, the Portman was a miserable little drinking den full of dead-eyed regulars. Its floorboards were bare and scuffed, and its walls were yellow from nicotine even though the smoking ban had forced drinkers to puff out in the wind and cold for several years now.

The boozer was almost completely empty, but even so Connor barely noticed the bespectacled figure sitting at the bar reading the *Daily Herald*. He ordered himself a pint.

'Are you not buying a beer for me?'

The reporter turned to size up his inquisitor.

A slim, middle-aged man wearing a blue pullover and casual trousers, best described as slacks, smiled back at him and offered his hand as a welcome. 'Colin Harris is my name, and you must be Elvis. Actually, I'll have a glass of Chablis, stopped drinking beer the last time I got out of jail, puts too much on the gut.' With that remark he clasped the remains of his beer belly.

Connor screwed up his face and replied, 'With all due respect I don't think this is the type of establishment that sells wine, never mind Chablis.'

Harris burst out laughing and shouted to the ageing barmaid, 'Hey, Mary, two glasses of my usual – in fact better make it the whole bottle.'

The large, tattooed barmaid produced an expensive bottle of Chablis.

Harris gave Connor a playful, but painful, dig in the ribs. 'Les Preuses Chablis Grand Cru – about £160 a bottle. Don't you know what they say about never judging a book by its cover?'

He had a point. Colin 'The Hitman' Harris looked nothing like Connor imagined, with his John Lennon spectacles and an almost sheepish demeanour which gave him an air of respectability you wouldn't expect of one of Glasgow's most feared gangland enforcers. Then again, Connor figured that was probably part of Harris's success – the fact that no one would give him a second's notice before it was too late.

Harris leaned fractionally closer and asked, 'Do you want something else to go with your wine? A line, perhaps?' The gangster asked as casually as if he was offering Connor a cigarette.

'No thanks, alcohol is my only poison,' the journalist replied. Connor had never tried cocaine or any drugs for that matter and he hated what it did to his fellow hacks on nights out. By ten o'clock, after several trips to the toilets, Connor could no longer hold anything resembling a meaningful conversation with his colleagues. He remembered seeing the tell-tale white powder in the nostrils of a once glamorous PR and couldn't for the life of him figure out why a woman pushing sixty would need cocaine in her life.

Connor simply found drugs boring. He'd grown up with them, as his mum and uncles and their friends had all been cannabis smokers. He'd listen to their wild claims that dope was the only non-addictive drug then watch them get all antsy and narky when they didn't have any. And, worst of all, he had to listen to the hashheads talking shit. They thought they were so rebellious and daring because they lived their lives in a fug of dope smoke, evading the law, as if the law really cared that much about them. To them, everyone else was a 'normal'. Thirty years on, Connor would have a quiet chuckle to himself at how the lives of the once young and trendy drugged-up ideologists had panned out. One uncle now made a living driving a taxi, the other a courier van, and one of his mum's closest friends sold kitchen units.

They still got high every night, while Connor had gone on to enjoy a varied and interesting career without the need to get high. He eyeballed Harris and added, rather unnecessarily, 'Personally, I think drugs are for losers, whether you're loaded or living in a council house. You're still a loser.'

Harris stared at Connor in silence. His own £250,000-a-year coke use was well known, although he'd kicked the habit long ago. Fortunately, he decided he quite liked the fact that Connor wasn't afraid to speak his mind in front of him. Harris was surrounded by quite enough yes men. The gangster placed a hand on Connor's shoulder and said, 'You know, two years ago I'd have had you wasted for calling me a loser, but now I'm clean I know you're absolutely correct. It saddens me to see people, policemen or prostitutes, hooked on drugs.' Drug abuse may sadden Harris, but it had also made him immensely rich as one of the country's biggest drug suppliers.

Connor felt he'd pushed his luck far enough and let Harris's last remark pass without comment. After all, he was dealing with a man whose ruthlessness and violence were legendary.

Harris had once been charged with the murder of the son of Glasgow's Godfather, Mr Ferguson, an 'untouchable'. He had stood trial at the High Court in Glasgow accused of killing Ferguson Junior in what turned into one of Scotland's longest running murder cases, only for the charge to be found 'not proven' – that unique verdict in Scottish law which means the prosecution have failed to convince the jury. But everyone knew Harris did it. Ferguson Senior promised to pay a million pounds if Harris was taken out. It was suspected he wouldn't survive a week after walking free.

However, that was a decade ago. Ferguson Senior had died from old age and a broken heart, never having avenged the death of his son. Harris had survived and flourished. He'd become an unlikely publishing phenomenon after the release of his first of four autobiographies, based around his violent life. There was talk of a movie deal, too, as the public's appetite for gangster stories seemed insatiable. Ironically, Harris's books were all ghost-written by his former social worker turned true crime writer Ron McLeod, who liked to call himself Big Mac. Critics claimed that 'writer' was too strong a term for Big Mac. While the books would never be literary classics, the neds lapped them up, queuing for hours at book signings to meet their gangster hero. For many, Harris's life stories were the first books they'd read since school.

But Scotland was still a small pond, in which writers struggled to scrape a living. His book earnings could in no way account for the top-of-the-range Jaguar XJ parked conspicuously outside the Portman's door.

Connor followed Harris to a booth with torn red vinyl seats. Harris poked at one of the holes with his index finger and sighed, 'This place has seen better days, but it was my dad's favourite. And no one hassles me in here. I can't be bothered with the young crew who want a scrap just so they can boast they took on Colin 'The Hitman' Harris.' He winked. 'Although I'd have done the same myself at their age. To be young and daft again, eh?' His demeanour changed as he leaned over the table to face Connor. 'Now, here are the rules of engagement. You can ask me anything you like, but some things I will not answer, in case I incriminate other people or, more importantly, myself.'

It was a strange opening salvo, for it was Harris who had summoned Connor and anyway there was only one question anyone, including the authorities, wanted Harris to answer: Did you kill Ferguson Junior?

Harris paused for a moment then plainly stated, 'This serial killer you've been writing about, I need to meet him.'

'Ha, join the queue.'

But Harris wasn't laughing. Instead an eerie look had fallen over him, half calm, half volcanic anger. Connor suspected he'd just glimpsed the real Harris, the one so many of his victims had encountered.

When Harris eventually spoke again he had regained his composure. 'No, you don't understand. I really need to meet him. He just murdered my sister.'

17

UNDERGROUND, OVERGROUND

April was determined to do more than just sit on the cat again as she slumped in her favourite chair at home. As usual, her mind wandered randomly and she decided it was time to sieve through the clutter of her spare room cum guest bedroom. She discovered an unopened box in the corner with a sewing machine inside and remembered how she had planned to start making curtains for herself, her daughter and friendly neighbours.

April had hoped to have become 'the talk of the area', seeing people nudge each other out the corner of her eye and whisper, 'There's that April Lavender, not only is she a famous journalist, but she can also run up a fine set of drapes.' That plan came to an abrupt halt the day she went to price some curtain material. The shop had wanted ninety pounds. April flounced off, later telling a friend over a bottle of wine, 'I could get a pair of ready-made curtains for the same price – we have a lot to thank these sweat shops for.'

Since then the sewing machine had lain abandoned and unloved in the spare room, along with the fondue set and the electronic corkscrew still in its box with its ten-page instruction booklet. Although no cork, however stubborn, had ever managed to get in the way of April and a wine bottle's contents.

But, one box she was determined to get to grips with was her Netbook, a mini laptop that had suddenly become all the rage. She lifted the flimsy-looking machine out of the packaging and set about powering it up. That had been the easy part as it came with just one cable, which plugged into a power socket. April attempted to flick through the instruction manual, but it was all Greek to her. In actual fact, it was all Greek, as she had accidentally flicked to the G for Greek section instead of GB for Great Britain.

She thought about calling Connor, but knew she would got his usual response of, 'I'm not the bloody IT desk, April.' Her second best option would be her daughter, but Jayne could be just as sarky as Connor. She tried her anyway.

'Okay, you've got a Netbook, which should be easy enough. So, who's your internet provider?' Jayne asked.

'Eh?'

'Who supplies your broadband? BT? Virgin Media? Sky?'

'I don't know.'

'Okay, forget that. What you need is a dongle,' Jayne said, only to be met by guffaws of laughter down the line.

'A *womble*?' April said through tears of mirth, before singing the song to the 1970s telly favourites, 'Remember you're a Womble.'

'Yes, Mum,' Jayne snapped, 'what you really need to do is plug in a fucking Womble. Look, no offence, but life's too short to help with your laptop. Why don't you enrol in a class or something, where they teach technophobes like you how to work computers? I've got to go. I'll speak to you and your Womble later.'

April repacked her Netbook – minus a Womble – and put it back in the spare room.

Connor had left the Portman that evening buzzing from a mix of good wine and the adrenaline rush he got each time he had a good story. Harris had only parted with his mum's address on the promise that she would be handled with kid gloves by the best in the business. Unfortunately, Connor couldn't get the best in the business on the phone. 'She's probably bloody eating again,' he cursed.

He wasn't far off the mark. April had been unable to find her vibrating mobile from within the depths of her bulging handbag in time as she attempted to juggle a biscuit and a cup of tea at the same time. When she eventually found it, Connor had already left a voicemail. Unable to remember how to access her messages, she called Connor while eating her second biscuit.

He told her, 'First thing in the morning I need you to get to the Red Road flats to interview Colin Harris's mum.'

April wasn't the best with names, but after a second the penny dropped, 'Oh, the Hitman chappy – okay.'

'Jackie McIvor was Harris's half-sister. It'll be a splash. But we need the mum's reaction, too. I've already cleared it with the Weasel and told the picture desk too.'

'Right, first thing,' April promised, brushing the crumbs from her Hob Nob from her cleavage.

'Oh, and, April,' Connor added, 'will you please do me the courtesy of not eating while you're on the phone to me.'

April laughed and hung up. She checked her handbag, which contained several full notepads and pens – half of them dried up and useless – and left it by the door, attempting to be organised and ready for an early morning exit.

She was intrigued by how this whole investigation was panning out. Whoever had killed Jackie not only had the police on his tail, but now Scotland's most lethal hitman. It would be yet another exclusive splash from the Special Investigations unit.

18

THAT'LL BE THE DAEWOO

April sat in her purple Daewoo estate urging the engine to heat up to take the chill off the morning air. Almost every panel on the ageing car, from the doors to the bumpers, the hatchback and somehow even the roof, was either dented, scuffed or scratched, for April was a truly awful driver who handled any vehicle like a dodgem.

Her main problem was that she was barely able to see over the steering wheel. She was blissfully unaware that Daewoo steering wheels were adjustable and that hers was set to the highest level. She also had no concept of the width or length of the car, meaning she'd always take up two parking spaces in the office car park, usually after rattling her Daewoo off a concrete pillar or someone else's bumper first.

When she drove, April focused exclusively on the road ahead, paying no attention whatsoever to her peripheral vision. Connor had accidentally discovered this when he saw April out driving one Sunday afternoon. He had pulled up alongside her car on the M8 to give his colleague a friendly wave as she made one of her twice-weekly visits to IKEA, the giant Swedish furniture store at Braehead, on the outskirts of Glasgow. Despite sounding his horn, April's eyes did not once flicker in his direction.

Connor decided to drive behind her, flashing his high beam lights. Again, April refused to take her tunnel-like vision off the road to glance in her rear-view mirror, although the beam from Connor's Audi was so strong it illuminated the entire interior of April's car even in broad daylight.

Intrigued, he tailed her all the way to the IKEA car park, where he pulled up beside her and waited. She still hadn't noticed him. When she finally got out, after applying another thick layer of lip gloss, April greeted Connor with a whoop of surprise. 'Oh, it's yourself. Are you coming in for the meatballs, you can't beat IKEA meatballs.'

'April,' Connor asked, 'I've been following you for miles, blaring my horn, flashing my lights.'

She let out her trademark cackle. 'Ach, when I get in my car it's "Thunderbirds are go!"'

But this morning April was trying to negotiate the satellite navigation system her daughter had bought her for Christmas, to find her way to the mum of the murdered prostitute Jackie McIvor. She hated the sat nav and the way it 'barked instructions' at her, complaining, 'I never let any of my husbands speak to me that way, so I'm certainly not about to let a little black box talk to me like that. And, anyway, how would you know the way around Glasgow with an American accent?'

At that moment, another forceful Yankee drawl was speaking in a car only a few miles from April. And Osiris was letting every positively charged word of encouragement sink in. He knew time was short. His next moves would have to be swift, which meant risk, but he knew he could do it.

'Visualise your goal,' whined the nasal voice of the life coach, 'so that you can almost reach out and touch them. Think of nothing else but success – failure is not an option – then go for it. You will succeed only if you have no doubt in your head.'

The CD ended. Osiris gripped the steering wheel of the Ford Mondeo and stared longingly into the distance. Like a light switch being flicked on it became clear to him exactly what he must do next.

19

OLD JEANNIE

April took the lift to the twenty-third floor of the Red Road flats – the towering 1960s monstrosities that dominated the skyline of the city.

Glasgow City Council was slowly trying to make amends for this social housing experiment borrowed straight out of the handbook of Stalinist Russia. It was rehousing the residents of the twenty-four-storey vertical housing estates, with plans to eventually pull down the concrete monoliths.

But old Jeannie was staying put. Despite the lifts rarely working, which meant she was virtually a prisoner in her own home for most of the week, she didn't seem to mind, as long as she had her Sky telly, her soaps, and her weekly dance at the nearby Alive and Kicking social club, where pensioners got a boogie and a free lunch. In fact, the only time the council got an ear-bashing from old Jeannie was when the lifts failed on a Wednesday lunchtime forcing her to miss her weekly social encounter.

The eighty-two-year-old had three children to three different men and used to joke she was ahead of her time from all the young single mums pushing prams around the estate. But she had outlived two of her kids including her eldest son who had drunk himself to death four years previously and now her only daughter, who had been found murdered just days ago. That left her youngest son Colin, who had been a constant source of worry to her all his life. And with good cause.

Colin Harris had rarely been out of trouble. She had lost count of the number of times he'd turned up at her door as a young man, covered in blood. She always kept a wardrobe full of spare clothes for him, knowing he'd need to burn the ones he'd arrived in to destroy the evidence.

She had frowned and voiced her extreme displeasure each time he'd asked her to 'look after something' for him. That something usually being a handgun. But she told herself that it wasn't her precious Colin's fault. The other boy must have been asking for it. Or attacked him first. All her life she'd been making excuses for her son. She knew he was smart, very smart; it was just unfortunate that his temper got the better of him at times.

And don't get her started on 'the polis'. They were always on his case. Taking him in for questioning about this that and the next thing. But that was a long time ago. Her Colin was a businessman now and very successful he was, too. She hated the newspapers for always branding him a 'gangster' or a 'gun runner' or that horrible nickname 'The Hitman'. And why did they always have to drag up his past when he'd been acquitted of the murder of Ferguson Junior? Didn't that fat bastard have it coming anyway, the way he always used to bully her son and call him names and batter him? Ferguson Junior used to strut around the area as if he owned the place just because of who his dad was. But Colin Harris was afraid of no man, just as Jeannie had raised him to be.

April knocked again on Jeannie's door. She could hear the telly on so she knew someone was in.

Eventually a croaky voice demanded, 'Whit dae ye want?' from behind a reinforced door that wouldn't have looked out of place in a bank vault.

April got into gear, pleading, 'I'm here to speak to you about your daughter, Mrs Harris. I'm a reporter and I want to help find her killer. I really need to talk to you. Tell me what she was like. Tell me so someone will read about your loss and will shop the bastard who did this terrible thing to your wee girl.'

April may have had many faults, but she knew how to talk to a grieving mother. She'd been one herself, although she never revealed anything more than the fact that she'd lost a son. A female doctor had once told her she needed to 'open up' and 'get her feelings out in the open'. April had replied, 'I can only function by keeping it bottled, you daft bitch.' But her loss gave her a kinship instantly recognised by other grieving mothers.

The two women remained silent, separated by a few inches on

either side of the door. The deadlock was broken by a strange muffled sound. April tilted her ear towards the door. The sound she could hear was of an old woman crying, followed by the heavy clunks of numerous locks.

April had succeeded once again. She was over the threshold, albeit unwittingly aided and abetted by the ruthless Colin Harris, who'd called Jeannie half an hour before the reporter had arrived, telling his mum to 'let in the crazy old cow' when she came knocking at the door.

The *Daily Herald* front page headline read:

HITMAN HARRIS – I'M COMING TO GET YOU
Gangster's chilling threat to serial killer.
Exclusive by APRIL LAVENDER and CONNOR PRESLEY.

And underneath:

FEARED GANGSTER COLIN HARRIS last night promised to avenge the death of Jackie McIvor after revealing the murdered prostitute was his half-sister.

The street worker's body was found just five miles from the body of jewellery tycoon Selina Seth this week, sparking fears that a serial killer is on the loose.

But Harris – one of Scotland's leading underworld figures – has vowed to find his sister's killer BEFORE the police.

Harris – nicknamed The Hitman – said: 'My Jackie had her problems. I tried everything I could to get her off the drugs. But no one deserves to be attacked like that and dumped by the roadside like a dead dog. Whoever did this better hope and pray the police find them before I do.'

On the first two pages inside were similar threats by Harris, followed by a round-up of the case so far from Selina's death, her husband Martin's failed suicide attempt, the discovery of Jackie McIvor's body and DCI Crosbie's insistence that he was not after a serial killer and was treating the murders as two separate cases.

But it was April's interview with old Jeannie which stole the show. The pictures of the old woman, floods of tears streaming down her wrinkled face, while clutching a picture of her dead daughter, would have touched the coldest of hearts.

April expertly told Jeannie's story, that of an uneducated woman born into poverty, who had tried her best to raise three children and was now left with only one. Jeannie mentioned nothing of her years helping to cover up Colin's crimes. Instead, Jeannie had made Colin out to be the victim and insisted he was only trying his best for a better life. She brushed aside his violent nature with a memorable quote: 'It's dog eat dog around here – only the toughest survive.'

As for Jackie, Jeannie spoke about her lifelong battle with drugs. How she had 'leathered her' after catching her smoking a joint at the tender age of nine. 'But no matter how many times I battered her, Jackie just couldn't stay away from the drugs. In the end I just let them do them at home. I'd rather she did drugs under my watchful eye than in some drug den.'

April's report gave the readers a snapshot of a world many had never experienced and would never want to. It gave perfect balance to the chilling threat from Colin Harris on the front page. April and Connor's reporting had wiped the floor with the opposition. They may have been a generation apart, but the reporters had gelled into one formidable unit.

This was not what the Weasel and Bent had planned at all.

Osiris was not in a positive state of mind.

He had just read Connor and April's exclusive, which contained a threat directed towards him. 'Who the hell does this Colin Harris think he is?' he thought to himself. 'Another self-styled hardman gangster?'

But his bravado didn't match the true way he was feeling. Osiris was worried. The serial killer coverage gave Osiris a mystique he didn't truly deserve. He was a most efficient killer all right, but a cowardly and opportunistic one. His victims were the vulnerable: nearly always prostitutes high on drugs. Some even let him strangle them to begin with, as many of their clients liked that sort of thing. By the time they realised this customer planned to be their last, it was usually too late.

But Osiris did not like tackling men. He had murdered one male – a skinny little runt he'd met in a bar in London's Soho.

Like many homophobes, Osiris thought he despised gay men, when really all he was doing was attacking his own inner turmoil. The weakling had been easily strangled, but Osiris hadn't even bothered to add him to his kill total, because he'd tried to bury the memories of their sexual encounter. He'd also been very drunk at the time – the early 1980s, long before the days of CCTV. He couldn't even remember where he'd left the stranger's body, but it was most probably in the lane where they'd had sex.

But that was the old Osiris. The new Osiris was a professional killer – and ultra careful. For his next move, he had no choice but to throw caution to the wind. Unplanned kills left a lot to chance and exposed him to the very real risk of being caught. That's why his job, which involved long periods travelling around the country, was ideal for his nocturnal pursuits. But the next stage of his plan made him nervous as hell as he planned to meet Selina Seth's widower.

'Why the fuck didn't we know that dirty prossie was Harris's half-sister?' squawked the Weasel later that morning. The editor was in his usual pose, fingers resting on his chin in a V-shape, scowling at April and Connor. 'I mean, someone must have known. How are we only finding out now?' he prattled on in mock outrage.

April and Connor knew the bollocking was manufactured, an attempt to make them look bad. April decided to go for it. 'Jackie didn't trade on her brother's name as she was scared it would scare punters off. Who'd want to have sex with the sister of one of Glasgow's most notorious gangsters? Anyway we've found out now, before every other paper. At least Jackie turned tricks for money, what was Selina's excuse?' she added pointedly.

If the editor heard her, it didn't seem to register. 'Well, I think we should stay on Harris's case, stake him out, as he'll have more chance of finding his sister's killer than the Keystone Cops. I'll organise the stakeout.'

And with that it was clear the meeting was over. It was also apparent that the Weasel was taking over the running of the investigation. He couldn't risk the dynamic duo hitting the jackpot again. With no thank-you and no meaningful direction as to what Connor and April should do next the pair were dismissed.

Back in the broom cupboard, Connor moaned, 'Colin Harris had the best surveillance units from Strathclyde Police on his tail for months before his trial for murder and even they couldn't keep tabs on him. But now the Weasel thinks a scribbler and a snapper will be able to follow him about in a car as he tracks down a serial killer? I tell you, papers aren't what they used to be.'

'Spoken like an old pro,' observed April.

'But it's true. It used to be alcoholics and mad men – often both – at the top of the tree. They were insane but they were newspapermen at heart. They knew what they were doing and more importantly knew what their readers wanted. This new breed act the part, but if you look at the Weasel's role during this case from start to finish he's contributed absolutely nothing.' Connor could tell by the faraway look in April's eye that he'd lost his captive audience of one. 'Hungry?' he enquired, already knowing the answer.

'Bloody starving,' she replied.

'Come on then, lunch is on me. Then I really need to buy myself some running gear for the weekend.'

20

FIGHTING FIT

April normally found herself at a loose end at the weekends. She would go and see her daughter and granddaughter on Sundays, but today she planned to get in some serious selling on eBay. Her daughter had introduced her to it. Being what was termed a Type A personality, April instantly became hooked. She'd even forgiven Jayne for the username she'd given her, 'oldsoak69' and the password 'gordonsgin'.

April had never thought of herself as a woman with a drink problem. She didn't crave it in the mornings, and she didn't suffer from hangovers, although Connor insisted that was because she was permanently pickled. But April enjoyed a 'good drink', which in Scotland meant downing enough to fell an elephant.

She wasn't too fond of beer, but everything else was most definitely on the drinks menu: wine – red/white/rosé, she wasn't fussed. Whisky – any cheap supermarket blend would do. And gin and tonics had gone from being an exclusive summertime drink to an all-year-round tipple. The same for Pimms. And she quite liked a Bacardi Breezer of an evening, or a rum and Coke. And a cheeky wee voddie and fresh orange also went down a treat. So, really, with all that rattling around her well-stocked drinks cabinet she really couldn't object to the username.

She felt sorry that Jayne never enjoyed a drink the same way she had – maybe she'd be more relaxed if she had. Her daughter insisted that watching her mother boozing throughout her childhood had put her off. So worried had she been about her mother's alcohol consumption, Jayne had once videotaped April coming in from a boozy night out with her pal Flo. April and Flo had done a conga through the front door, then proceeded to perform a Highland fling together in the living room. The tape ended with April snoring loudly on the couch.

Instead of being shame-faced by her antics the following morning, April had clipped Jayne around the ear and warned her not to disrespect her mother in that way ever again. However, she had shunned drink altogether over the last few nights for her new addiction, hawking her wares on the online auction site.

After April had cleared out the clutter of her spare room her Womble-less Netbook had been the first to go. Amazingly it sold for just forty pounds less than she had paid for it as it was almost unused. She then decided to raid her loft, and swiftly decided that nothing was off limits from the old record player to some Jack Vettriano prints she hadn't got round to framing.

April was amazed there was a market for her old junk. Every second morning she had to make a stop at the post office to send various parcels on their way, while her bank account began to bulge.

April would bore Connor rigid with the details of her latest wheeling and dealing on a Monday morning in the broom cupboard. She'd told him last week how, 'My aunt Jessie had given me some fine bone china when I got married for the first time. It'd been too fancy to use as I was scared to break it. Well, you know how ham-fisted I am. I actually forgot I had it, but there it was, a complete twenty-four-piece dining set. £320 I got for that. Well, it's better off money in the bank than gathering dust in the attic.'

Disinterested, Connor had yawned and replied, 'The pawn shop would've given you the same and you wouldn't have had to fanny around with post and packaging.'

April had retorted, 'And just where is the fun in that?'

In a few weeks' time Connor would ask April to flog his Asics Gel-Kayano trainers for him on eBay. He would wear them only once after they'd served their purpose.

Connor had lied his way into the blue group of runners for the Great Scottish Run, having told the organisers he regularly ran half-marathons in one hour thirty-five. Being a journo from the country's biggest selling newspaper, they gave him a free entry. Now he found himself surrounded by 15,000 other eager souls on a bright Sunday morning in George Square, ready to pound 13.1 miles around the city.

Covering crime for the *Daily Herald* sometimes gave Connor a distorted view of society. In his world it was all knife and gun crime with revenge slashings and shootings, along with drugs and the highly organised criminals who supplied them. Elsewhere in the paper were stories of the country's increasing adult and childhood obesity, with warnings that we'd soon all be waddling around like fat Americans. But here was the very antithesis of all that. Thousands upon thousands of fit people, most of who were running for charitable causes. There was camaraderie about them, like one massive football team where everyone played for the same side. Connor liked how it made him feel, to be amongst good folk.

DCI Crosbie was thinking the exact same thought as he basked in the feeling of goodwill. Connor and Crosbie had a lot in common. They were the same age, where ambition has been replaced by weariness, but they also missed absolutely nothing.

It was Crosbie who spotted the reporter first. Like many coppers he never forgot a face, but this one was out of context and Crosbie couldn't place him at first. Then the penny dropped. 'The *Daily* cunting *Herald*. What does that fucking arsehole want?'

The crime reporter soon managed to manoeuvre into position alongside the detective. Without giving Connor even a sideways glance, Crosbie enquired, 'First time?'

Connor had been found out. 'How did you know?'

Crosbie turned ever so slightly towards Connor and smiled. 'Well, for starters, there's the spanking new trainers. Then you've left the price tag on your running top, and if you will forgive me for being overly personal, you also have a slight beer belly. I'm afraid you don't have to be Sherlock Holmes to figure out you haven't run a race since school sports day. Oh, and just a little aside, your picture by-line wasn't taken yesterday either.'

Connor had to laugh. He'd been well and truly busted. He hadn't run since school and his by-line pic was at least a decade old. But Crosbie's friendly demeanour gave him hope that he may be able to develop some sort of relationship with him. He took a gamble by giving the cop a taste of his own medicine.

'Okay. Well, I see a man who keeps himself to himself, who is bound by a sense of duty but hates the politics involved with his rank. Someone who has resisted recent promotion opportunities, because it takes him further away from solving crime and feeling the collar of bad guys. Someone who is determined to catch the killers of Selina Seth and, just as importantly, Jackie McIvor. And someone who hasn't had a chance lately to run nearly as much as he'd like.'

Crosbie turned to eyeball Connor again, staying momentarily silent. He eventually said, 'I would have told you to piss off until you said "killers" and not "killer". Glad to see you don't actually believe the guff your newspaper churns out.'

Crosbie knew he was being disingenuous to the *Daily Herald*, a paper he secretly liked. He'd also been reading Connor Presley's articles for years. He liked his style. His reports were always well informed and well written. Connor didn't tend to go in for flyers – when a grain of truth is spun up into something it's not. Some hacks didn't even start with anything as small as a grain.

In fact Crosbie had often wondered what it would have been like to be in Connor's shoes. Not that he would ever let the journo know that. 'Run with me,' he said warmly, before adding with a grin, 'and see how long you can keep up with the Glasgow polis.'

As Connor was pounding the streets of Glasgow, April Lavender was also about to indulge in a rare bout of exercise. She looked down at the spare tyres of fat that rippled out beyond her ample bosom, all covered by a straining layer of lilac-hued swimming costume and topped with a matching frilly hat. 'I look like the Sugar Plum Fairy,' she thought.

By any standards she was quite a sight. To make matters worse, April was also terrified of water, even though she would only be thrashing around in the shallow end. She felt better when she saw a fellow Sugar Plum Fairy self-consciously make her way into the pool.

'Glad to see I have another skinny supermodel for company,' April grinned.

Both women roared with laughter. 'Well, at least we're trying – got to give us Brownie points for that,' replied the stranger, before offering her hand and introducing herself. 'I'm Celia.'

'And I'm April. Pleased to meet you.'

With that the two new-found friends entered the shallows together, like a pair of hippos.

Osiris pushed his frame as far back into the driver's seat as he could.

The prostitute he'd picked up was clearly stoned. She fumbled at his belt buckle and zip, before lazily giving him oral sex. Osiris was barely aroused. He stroked the back of the prostitute's vulnerable neck, like a cat toying with its prey. She felt him stiffen considerably.

He loved the feeling of life or death he held in his hands. There were more reasons to kill her than not, but Osiris had bigger fish to fry. Osiris came, before grabbing a handful of the prostitute's hair and stuffing a twenty-pound note into her mouth. Her eyes widened with shock. He slapped her hard then snarled, 'Now fuck off, you slut, before I change my mind,' and pushed her roughly onto the street, where she scurried off like a frightened animal.

He always felt dirty after sex and cursed himself. 'Fucking whore – should have made her a mercy killing.'

The wheels of his red Mondeo spun wildly as he sped off into the night.

21

BORED STIFF

Connor walked through the doors of the Peccadillo café safe in the knowledge that April would be eating and baffling the waiting staff as usual. Even from a distance he could tell that his crime-fighting colleague was tucking into a particularly hearty breakfast. He sat down opposite her, and she immediately started speaking through mouthfuls of food. 'Oh, hello, how are …' Connor presumed she'd said 'you' but couldn't quite make it out as she sent speckles of half-chewed breakfast spraying in his general direction.

April talked with her mouth full a lot, partly because she ate continuously and partly because she was always so friendly with folk she treated them like family. Connor often had to transfer calls from April's daughter Jayne to her phone as both mother and daughter were incapable of remembering April's direct line. Jayne was usually eating at the same time as her mother on the opposite end of the phone, causing Connor to remark on more than one occasion how the apple hadn't fallen very far from the tree. Knowing the Lavender girls, they'd have eaten the apple, too.

April was in a particularly anxious mood this morning. 'Let me tell you what happened with Jayne this weekend. Well, you know how she and Jon are getting divorced …'

Connor tuned out. He'd heard every minute detail of Jayne and Jon's strung-out separation. He sat dead-eyed as April launched into the next boring chapter of 'he said that' and 'she did what'. It reminded Connor of his own childhood when his own parents had separated. Dad had left for a younger woman and seemed to be very happy with his new arrangement. Mum, on the other hand, made her sole reason for living the destruction of Dad's newfound happiness. Everything was used as a bargaining tool – birthdays, Christmases, holidays. All of them tinged with the sadness that can only be brought on by increasingly bitter parents who'd made Connor piggy-in-the-middle.

He didn't dwell much on his past – there was nothing but heartache there. Now, apart from his work, he lived his own life free of confrontation, partly because he'd never entered into a steady relationship. Sure, he'd had plenty of girls, but the thrill of the chase soon evaporated on the third or fourth night they slept together. Connor wasn't the type to blame his commitment-phobia baggage on his parents. As far as he was concerned his choices meant he was able to live the way he chose, and not having screaming matches every night was top of his agenda.

April gestured to pay her bill, but when they both went to stand up they grimaced simultaneously. Their weekend exercise had left them stiff as boards. April laughed, 'Look at the state of us – what a couple of old crocks.'

The Weasel didn't allow the Special Investigations unit the luxury of taking their jackets off before he began barking instructions at them in his charmless style. 'New week, same old serial killer on the loose.'

Connor corrected him. 'There are actually two killers on the loose.'

The Weasel continued as if Connor hadn't spoken. 'What did you find out from that plod, Crosbie?'

'Ah,' said Connor as if he'd only just remembered, 'that's something I need to speak to you and Bent about.'

The Weasel visibly bristled. Connor couldn't tell whether it was from his brazenness at requesting a meeting with the editor or the contemptuous use of his master's surname.

'Ten o'clock,' he snarled and slammed the broom cupboard door behind him.

Connor turned round to see April's eager face staring back at him.

'Gosh, this sounds exciting. What are we going to speak them about?' she beamed.

Connor stared at her ageing moon face in silence for a moment, before muttering under his breath, 'Different planet – she's on a different planet.'

Half an hour later, at precisely 9.59 a.m., the Weasel chapped impatiently on the broom cupboard's door, which was a first.

'I didn't think he knew how to knock,' said Connor. 'Let the bastards stew a few minutes more.' He giggled to himself.

April had just nipped off for one of her regular loo breaks, keeping Bent and the Weasel waiting even longer.

Connor decided to get the meeting started without her. April's flustered late arrival would irritate the fastidious Bent anyway. Striding purposefully into the editor's office he didn't bother with any pleasantries – none given, none received. Instead, he quickly outlined the subbed-down version of the conversation he'd had with Crosbie and the special request the DCI had made.

'And this flatfoot has promised us the exclusive? He won't go giving it to everyone else at the eleventh hour?' the Weasel snarled.

'Nope – doesn't like dealing with the press, but he seems to have liked our coverage, despite our front page linking the deaths of Seth and McIvor, which was a pile of crap, to paraphrase Crosbie. But he's willing to overlook that to work exclusively with us.'

Connor let his statement hang in the room knowing full well the two men before him had planned that front page together, despite Connor's insistence it was inaccurate. They were dumb-struck by his bluntness. Finally, Bent broke the tension. 'Well, I don't like it. I don't like it one bit. I think your DCI Crosbie plans to use us,' he said, spitting out the words. 'I think it's time the *Daily Herald* brought this killer to justice since the cops seem to be incapable of catching him.'

Connor protested, 'With all due respect, we have no place interfering with two murder investigations … It's not our job …'

The Weasel cut him off. 'We can interfere with whatever and whomever we want. We're the *Daily* Fucking *Herald*.'

Connor returned the Weasel's hostile glare. This guy was a caricature of how a news editor should be. His management technique had died out with dinosaurs like Fleet Street legend Kelvin MacKenzie, who bullied his staff for fun and once famously sacked the *Sun*'s astrologer with the opening gambit, 'You probably already know this,' then spent the following thirty years dining out on that same tale.

But here were two living, breathing throwbacks to that bygone era, only, as far as Connor was concerned, they were poor imitations. He was of the opinion that most people worked harder and better out of a desire to impress a boss who was fair, rather than one they feared. But this pair had read the Stick It Up Your Punter handbook too often and were already legends in their own minds. That's why they felt they could interfere with the country's biggest manhunt. They weren't the ones who had to suffer the fallout. They barely left the office and therefore fell into a familiar newspaper executive trait of living in a bubble.

Connor stood his ground with a little psychology of his own. 'Let's give Crosbie a try. If he fucks with us then we'll crucify him. He'll have to leave Scotland and the force – or both – if he turns us over.' This fighting talk was enough to placate the Weasel and Bent. Connor left just as April was about to enter the room. He grabbed her forearm and steered her back to their broom cupboard.

'What did I miss?' she whispered.

Connor shrugged. 'Only the latest comedy routine from Dumb and Dumber. But we've got work to do. You need to see Crosbie. He owes us one.'

'And what are you going to do?' she asked.

Connor put on his coat. 'I need to thank an old friend before it's too late.'

22

STICKS AND STONES

'*Here she comes, the tart with the heart.*' It was an unfair description of April Lavender, but then again Crosbie's inner monologue was never known for its fairness. '*What does a fifty-six-year-old pudding like her think dyeing her hair peroxide blonde looks like anyway? Mutton dressed as mutton is what. Pathetic.*'

Crosbie's self-dialogue may have been unkind, but his outward persona was the complete opposite. As long as the inner didn't become the outer, Crosbie felt he could handle it. He'd given up any notion of going to see the force's psychiatrist. This double murder investigation was eating up all of his work and spare time. His little problem would have to remain in check until both were solved.

As agreed with Connor, the detective planned to get one case wrapped up as quickly as possible with a little bit of assistance from April Lavender. DCI Crosbie turned on the charm. 'So nice to meet you, Miss Lavender. I've been reading your articles for years.'

She roared with laughter, and playfully slapped the cop's shoulder, saying, 'Oh, you do know how to make a lady feel old.'

They were sitting in Crosbie's office at Strathclyde Police Headquarters in Glasgow's Pitt Street. He poured her a tea and judged correctly that she wouldn't object to the three assorted biscuits he placed on her saucer. She ate two and pocketed the third 'for later'.

'So, how do you fancy turning detective for us?' Crosbie asked casually.

'Do I get a cop's pension?' April answered with a full mouth, firing a hail of crumbs in Crosbie's direction.

Crosbie adopted a more serious expression. 'I can't offer you that, but I can offer you an exclusive – the capture of Selina Seth's murderer.'

'I know you're not supposed to speak ill of the dead, but she was a ghastly woman, you know,' April said, digressing as usual.

'Even the ghastly deserve justice,' Crosbie offered, 'you fat fuck.' His grin remained fixed. He wasn't sure if he'd just called April Lavender of the *Daily Herald*'s Special Investigations team a 'fat fuck' to her face. If he had, she certainly hadn't seemed to notice.

'Okay dokey, I'm off to meet Martin Seth again. If he tries to kill me I hope your big strong policemen will be nearby at the ready?'

'Don't worry,' Crosbie reassured her, having regained his composure, 'we'll have you rigged up with all the state-of-the-art equipment.'

'Are you going to turn me into Robocop? Half human, half robot?' April giggled playfully.

'I'm sure we could arrange that.' He grinned as he moved towards his door to show April out.

As the ageing reporter swept past him, she stopped suddenly to place her hand gently on Crosbie's forearm. In barely more than a whisper, she said, 'Your Tourette's won't get any better by itself, you know. You need to get help. Insults have never bothered me – in my line of work I've been called far worse – but if you call your superior officer a "fat fuck" you're going to seriously damage your career.'

Crosbie's face turned crimson as April rooted around in her sizeable handbag until she found what she was looking for. 'Ah, my contacts book,' she said triumphantly. The moth-eaten old book had once been bound in black leather, but the colour had long been scuffed off to leave a sickly grey. The pages inside contained a mass of numbers written in various colours of ink, with several scored out to be replaced with newer numbers. Old dog-eared business cards were wedged randomly into the spine of the book.

Crosbie was convinced not even his forensic scientists would have been able to make head nor tail of this jumble of names and numbers.

But April whistled gleefully as she quickly flicked through the pages before declaring, 'Ah, here it is,' and handed Crosbie a faded business card, which read, 'WATT WILSON – A HEALTHY MIND MAKES FOR A HEALTHY BODY.' Surprisingly it didn't have any of the credentials he imagined were required for a psychiatrist, with no long line of letters after his name. April seemed to read his thoughts. 'Oh, he's not a real shrink, but he will fix you. He sorted me and my husbands during our divorces – all three of them,' she added with a cackle. And with that she waddled off to be greeted by Crosbie's trusted sergeant, leaving the detective alone with his thoughts.

'She may be a mad old bat, but she's right. I do need help.' This time it wasn't Crosbie's inner monologue doing the talking.

An hour later April arrived at the Seths' mansion, which somehow seemed to be suffering from Selina's loss. It looked older, more decrepit, from the withered vines to the overgrown lawn.

When widower Martin answered the door after letting April through the security system at the front gates, he looked like he'd rapidly gone downhill, too.

April held up two grande lattes she'd brought with her from Starbucks and said with a smile, 'Coffee, Martin? You look like you could do with a hit of caffeine.'

'Thanks,' he mumbled, greedily grasping the disposable cup as if for warmth, adding, 'I haven't got any tea or coffee left – or milk for that matter.'

'I thought as much,' April said. 'Then again, you've had so much on your mind, you poor thing.' She produced four bacon rolls wrapped in brown paper, which were already soaked through from grease and contained in a thin white plastic bag. 'One bacon roll is never enough, I say, and you look famished. To tell the truth I'm a bit peckish myself.'

Martin and April sat in silence as they feasted on the coffee and bacon rolls.

When they were finished Martin gave a satisfied burp, before apologising, 'Sorry, my stomach's not used to it. I haven't eaten anything in days.'

For less than a tenner's worth of hot food and drink, April had made a friend.

They stared out at the spectacular views across the Kelvin valley with the Forth and Clyde canal up to the Kilsyth hills.

'In the winter, Selina said they looked just like mini Alps,' Martin reminisced. 'My parents bought this place in 1967. They wouldn't recognise it now, right enough. Selina had it knocked down and rebuilt from scratch when we began earning money. There wasn't even any electricity pylons running through Dullatur when I was growing up here. Imagine that. We had unspoilt views to feast our eyes on every day.'

It was only natural Martin should regress to much happier times after his days of trauma. But April needed to haul him back to the present. 'You know, everyone thinks you murdered your wife. My editor, our readers and the cops. But I don't, Martin. I truly don't believe you killed Selina. Help me prove them wrong.'

Martin gazed at his feet for a long time. Eventually he said, 'What does it matter now? Everything is ruined.'

'Oh, but it does matter, Martin,' she added. 'It matters a lot. If not to you, then to your children. How is life going to be for them with their mother killed and their father locked up for her murder?'

Martin began to weep. Slowly at first, with just a few tears staining his cheeks. But they soon made way to great howls of pain as Martin finally set free his agony.

April had been here many times before. She'd always had a way of tugging at folk's heartstrings long before she joined newspapers. Most people do feel better after bawling their eyes out, although she hadn't allowed herself to cry in years. She knew only too well if she opened those floodgates she would never be able to stop.

The sobs finally grew further and further apart. April discreetly switched on her voice recorder and placed it on the coffee table beside them. This was for April's own benefit, as every word said had already been recorded by a wireless transmitter, which was placed in her ample handbag – the microphone disguised as a peacock brooch on her jacket. 'Now's the time, Martin. Tell me what really happened.'

23

THE IM-PATIENT

Badger was holding court as usual, cigarette in hand, telling a mixture of old stories peppered with a colourful mixture of obscenities.

Connor couldn't help looking at him from a distance through admiring eyes. What was it about this foul-mouthed, cantankerous old sod that left such a lasting impression on all who knew and worked with him?

As Connor approached, Badger burst into his familiar greeting, chanting 'El-vis, El-vis – give us "Blue Suede Shoes".'

'You know,' Connor said in reply, 'one day I might just do that and then you'll be sorry.'

Badger's raucous laugh made way to a hacking cough. 'Come here, lad,' he eventually managed to splutter, before hugging Connor roughly. It was an awkward embrace with the younger reporter bent over his mentor's wheelchair. Badger whispered in his ear in a conspiratorial tone, 'I'm gubbed, son. My tea's out, but don't start blubbing yet. I've got to give those daft cunts over there some hope.' He motioned over his shoulder to various members of his family, who had assembled outside the main entrance of Gartnavel hospital, on Glasgow's Great Western Road.

Badger's wife Rita squeezed Connor tightly, kissed his cheeks and said, 'I'm so glad you've come – you've made Russell's day.'

'Right,' Badger announced returning to his bullish ways, 'I'm fed up with all the tears and snotters around here. I've been given six months to live and I'm not going to spend it looking at your greetin' faces. Elvis, push me over to that bench to give some of these poor sods a seat. Don't worry about me – I've brought my own.'

Connor found the lever to release the wheelchair's brakes and pushed Badger slowly over the twenty feet of hospital pavement to a row of benches. But with every crack and pebble the chair passed over, Badger winced agonisingly in pain.

'Careful, you twat,' he snapped. 'If I wanted to be handled as roughly as this I'd have stayed in the ward.'

Connor was no medical expert, but he thought his mentor's six-month life sentence was extremely optimistic, reasoning that if he had lost the power of his legs, then the cancer must surely have already spread.

'You know,' Badger said, his smile replacing his scowl, 'the doctors haven't told me to stop smoking. I thought that'd have been the first thing to go. "Now, Mr Blackwood, you must give up the ciggies since you have tumours growing in both lungs." But nope, nothing, not even a ticking off. Can you believe that?' He fired up another cigarette.

Connor never ceased to be amazed by the West Coast of Scotland's reckless attitude towards health. The region had consistently come top of the binge-drinking, coronary heart disease and lung cancer leagues for the whole of Europe and no matter how much money the government pumped into it, the statistics just got steadily worse. He suspected that many Glaswegians were secretly proud of the statistics – at least the country was top of something. But it always made grim reading for Connor. In the city's worst postcodes, life expectancy was just forty-eight years of age. Some developing nations could expect to live longer than that.

Connor gave a wry smile. 'Well, I guess it's a little too late to quit the ciggies now.' Although he dared not show it, inwardly Connor was grieving over his stricken mentor. His time left on the planet would be short. Connor hoped his final days wouldn't be spent in pain. He already looked like a bag of bones.

'Too fucking true,' Badger offered. 'The strange thing is I haven't missed the drink. Weird that, eh?'

Unbeknown to Connor, Badger had already been in hospital for a week when he received the call from Rita. She had told him bluntly how the doctors hadn't given him long to live, six months at most. That was clearly a lie, probably told because everyone – including the terminally ill – needed hope.

After the phone call Connor had wept as he hadn't wept before. Not even the death of his grandparents had triggered such an emotional response. He just couldn't imagine life without Badger. His mentor had always been there for him, whether it was for help and advice on a story, or just for a chinwag. They had been inseparable at the *Daily Herald*, with Connor accompanying Badger on his many fag breaks, even though the younger man never smoked. The age gap was fifteen years, but they seemed the only ones who were oblivious to it. As the exclusive splashes continued to roll in for the pair, professional jealousy and resentment set in with a small core of staff. They began spreading wicked rumours of a gay affair – why else would a haggard old hack be hanging around with a handsome upstart?

The gossip stopped abruptly one day when Badger suddenly excused himself from the smoking shed regulars to slam a passing reporter against the outside wall of the *Daily Herald* building. With barely concealed fury, Badger had gone eyeball to eyeball with the understandably frightened reporter and warned him that if he spread any more malicious rumours about himself and Connor then his wife would somehow find out he'd been 'screwing one of the telesales girls'.

The reporter had made a feeble attempt to deny everything, before his shoulders visibly sagged. He'd been caught bang to rights by an old journalist who had simply used his reporting skills – mixed with hints of menace and violence – to find the source of the gay rumours. With his target firmly in his sights he then set about digging up some dirt on the man.

That had been the easy part. Over a coffee with the editor's PA Moira – who had been on the *Daily Herald*'s staff as long as Badger – he had begun his conversation with, 'I need your help with this cunt, McKay.' Half an hour later he left armed with the name of McKay's mistress and how the gossipmonger had been warned about putting meals and hotel stays for his illicit affair on expenses.

Like a true gentleman, Badger had escorted Moira back to her desk, before kissing her on both cheeks saying, 'You are a darling, my dear.' The fact that Badger and Moira had once had a steamy, illicit affair of their own twenty years ago was neither here nor there.

That afternoon, as the unfortunate McKay was being slammed into the concrete wall of the building, a large and extravagant bouquet of flowers was delivered to the desk of one Miss Moira McMillan. Paid for on Badger's expenses. The whole episode had only enhanced the ageing hack's already formidable reputation.

But soon his stories would be all people would have to remember him; what they forgot about his career would be stored electronically in the archive. The next time his name appeared in the newspaper he once loved it would be no more than a three-paragraph filler mentioned on page two about his passing.

But that was all to come.

Connor laughed and smiled as Badger retold tales of old outside Gartnavel's Beatson cancer unit before a nurse was sent to retrieve her patient at dusk. Connor wondered how many more sunsets Badger would see. His final words to Connor before being wheeled away were, 'Did my Crosbie tip help you out, son?'

'It did, Badg, it did.'

That's all the dying reporter needed to know as he disappeared back into the ward with a huge smile stretched across his gaunt face.

24

THE CONFESSION

Osiris had finished another meeting over lunch with yet another transport boss, Stevie Holt, in the Bullion Bar in Edinburgh. The double murder stories had moved off the front pages of the newspapers as there was nothing left to report. Osiris knew that would all change within the next forty-eight hours.

'When you heading back south?' Stevie asked.

'Tomorrow, I reckon. Thursday the latest. I've got a few loose ends to tie up but I want to beat the Friday traffic.'

Osiris actually didn't mind heavy traffic. Sitting in jams gave him more time to listen to his self-help CDs. He enjoyed them most after a successful kill. He felt he could really relate to every sentence about positive energy when a plan had come off.

Now he needed a few more pieces – and players – to fall into place. He was certain that once that was achieved he would have completed several of his 'goals'.

He was about to make Martin Seth an offer he couldn't refuse.

Crosbie's inner monologue remained unusually silent as he listened intently to the conversation between April and Martin Seth, which he was hearing broadcast live from the surveillance equipment. What he heard disturbed him greatly.

April had been at her persuasive best, squeezing every last drop of information from her interviewee, then going over each fact and timeline again. But the alarm bells were ringing. Something just wasn't right. Martin Seth still wasn't telling the truth. All Crosbie's experience, training and plain gut instinct told him Martin was lying. Strange, considering Martin Seth had just confessed to murdering his wife.

* * *

April was having similar thoughts. Like Crosbie she'd spent her whole career interviewing people from all walks of life – and she knew bullshit when she heard it. But what to do? She had a confession in the bag. She needed to speak to Connor before facing the Weasel or Crosbie.

That wasn't going to be possible. No sooner had the electronic gates of the Seths' mansion closed behind her, an unmarked police car flashed its headlamps, summoning April to pull over.

The detective got out of the passenger door and invited April into his car. 'So what do you think of Martin's confession, you stupid bitch?' is what Crosbie heard himself ask, but hoped he'd managed to censor the offensive remark in time. His fixed grin became almost painful as he prayed he hadn't once again insulted one of Scotland's premier journalists.

'I'm not so sure,' April replied.

'Phew, got away with it again,' Crosbie thought with relief. But his moment of calm was shattered when April added with a smile, 'And who are you calling a stupid bitch?' Crosbie had been caught out again. 'Did you go and see Watt Wilson?' she asked.

'No, not yet, but I will. I'll call him today, I promise,' Crosbie said shamefaced.

'Right, what are we going to do about Martin? He didn't kill Selina, so that means he's covering up the real killer's identity, which is very, very strange. I mean, why would he do that?'

Crosbie played back the recording on his digital receiver, which had captured every word transmitted from April's brooch microphone. Martin's voice filled the inside of the silver Mercedes. 'She'd been cheating on me … I'd been humiliated one time too many … I was the brains behind Seth International … She got all the credit and nearly drove us under with all those stupid celebrities she thought were her friends.'

'It's a plausible motive, pity it's not true,' Crosbie stated, adding, 'We have Martin's mobile phone records from the day she was killed. He was at his parents' house with his kids. All of them have been questioned, and even the six-year-old said his daddy took him to school that morning. My pathologist places the time of Selina's death at around 9 a.m. The exact time

Martin was on the school run. So why the cover-up? Any ideas, cow face?'

April and DCI Crosbie sat in silence, mulling over the confession compared to the facts. She had come to find the barrage of insults from this high-ranking police officer amusing, especially when she let him know his inner conscience had escaped again.

'I'll need to interview him once more,' she said, 'lay the facts on the table that I know he was nowhere near the crime scene, and see if he's more forthcoming. And since you're now reduced to farmyard insults, if I'm an old cow, then you must be a cock.'

Crosbie sighed, 'I'll phone your witch doctor now, fatso.'

April laughed, 'This bulk doesn't maintain itself, you know. I am absolutely starving. I need to eat *now*.'

25

LOOK INTO MY EYES

Watt Wilson lived in the lower conversion of a once grand Victorian mansion in Cathkin Road on the city's Southside. He had carefully decorated his home cum business premises in the original style, with a grandfather clock gently chiming in the study and walls lined with row upon row of leatherbound journals.

His bald head, half-moon spectacles, tweed jacket with leather elbow patches and brogues gave him the air of an elderly scholar. But Watt was no doctor. Far from it. In fact, he hadn't bothered to read the many books that gave such a grand air to his study. The truth was, Watt was nothing more than a showman – a stage hypnotist, performing cheap parlour tricks in town halls across the country. He had once made a good living from it back in the late 1960s when hypnotists were all the rage, but his stage career had been cut short when one night a member of the audience – who it turned out had a history of mental illness – was hypnotised on stage by the great Watt Wilson.

Her schizophrenia had been suppressed by a cocktail of strong medication, but once under Watt's spell her darker side was suddenly set free. She had produced a kitchen knife from her bag and repeatedly stabbed the unfortunate Wilson to within an inch of his life. The attack had made front pages a long time ago. Since then Watt had reinvented himself as a doctor of the mind. He stopped short of calling himself a psychiatrist lest he feel the full wrath of the Psychiatric Council of Great Britain as he didn't have a single psychiatric qualification.

He had gone back to his old ways, hypnotising patients. But instead of asking them to drop their trousers for the amusement of a drunken theatre audience, he instilled them with positive thoughts.

His 'happy hypnosis' sessions, as he called them, proved successful enough for his popularity to spread by word of mouth. Apparently there wasn't a 'mind matter' that the great Watt Wilson couldn't resolve with around a dozen sessions – at fifty pounds each – on his velvet-covered chaise-longue.

'Depressed housewife? Never mind, dear, just be grateful for what you've got,' would be the message that Watt would repeatedly chant while they were under hypnosis.

His methods worked … to a point. His clients certainly left Watt's sessions feeling better about themselves, but his lack of professional training became apparent whenever one of his patients returned with their existing problem unresolved. For his hypnosis merely opened a can of worms for the more complicated cases.

Like the one who had just walked through the door.

Crosbie hadn't identified himself as a police officer, but Watt recognised a copper when he saw one. The dope parties he'd attended in the 1960s were prone to 'busts' by loutish police officers with an appetite for violence. All those old feelings of fear and loathing came back when Watt set eyes on the officer of Her Majesty's Constabulary.

'A friend recommended you,' Crosbie said curtly as he took off his jacket and placed it neatly on the chaise-longue.

'Well,' Watt replied with a well-rehearsed speech, 'that's the best recommendation of all. How can I help you?'

Crosbie shattered Watt's routine with a chilling demand. 'You can start by dropping the professor act, you stage hypnotist cunt, and find me a cure.'

Watt's heart sank. Not only did he hate his past catching up with him, but he already knew he had bitten off more than he could chew with this mysterious new patient.

26

BETWEEN A ROCK AND A HARD PLACE

April tucked into the café's Mega Breakfast Special, which she had repeatedly promised herself she would never order. It was like a super-sized Scottish breakfast and could easily have fed four. But, when under pressure, April ate even more than usual, which amounted to a whole lot of food.

She was made to feel even more guilty when the waitress Martel served it up by saying, 'Here's your heart attack on a plate.'

Connor appeared beside her, shaking his head ruefully, 'Good god, woman, even by your standards, that is one mighty plateful.'

From her customary full mouth, he managed to decipher the words, 'I don't care.'

'Well, just to give you the heads up, the Weasel's on the warpath because you didn't phone in yesterday. I don't mind you ignoring that idiot's calls, but why did you ignore mine? What the hell happened?'

April stopped chewing and sat in silence. Tears filled her eyes as she then explained how she believed Martin Seth's murder confession wasn't true, how DCI Crosbie had confirmed her instincts, and how she literally didn't know what to do next. 'I tried calling you, but got your voicemail. I didn't know what to tell the Weasel. He would have ignored my concerns and splashed it. Then Crosbie would have denied it. So I went swimming instead, which helped give me this healthy appetite.'

Without a hint of humour Connor said, 'There is nothing remotely healthy about your appetite. I tried calling you back, but your mobile must have been out of juice. You should have kept trying to reach me. We could have worked something out. You really are in the shit. The Weasel wants you up on a disciplinary.'

April dabbed her reddened eyes with the only corner of her napkin that wasn't stained with tomato sauce and egg yolk. 'I panicked,' she sobbed. 'I want to go back to speak with Martin Seth again, confront him with the facts and see what he says.'

Connor feared for April. She'd once told him how both her parents had suffered from Alzheimer's, explaining how her folks had 'forgotten everything – in the end they even forgot how to breathe'. He knew his colleague worried a lot about her possibly bleak future. He also knew many people had their own crosses to bear when it came to their genetic make-up. For some women it was the almost certain knowledge they would get breast cancer, after their mothers and grandmothers. Others walked around knowing their hearts were like ticking time bombs, with coronary heart disease running rife in their families despite good diets and healthy lifestyles.

For Connor it was Huntington's disease, a genetic disorder which affects the brain. He remembered vividly his gran's rapid mental decline. At first she had seemed fine, then one day she forgot to turn up at the school gates to collect him. He had been just five at the time, and two older girls had walked him back to his gran's home. She was sitting on the back porch having a cup of tea oblivious to her child-collecting duties.

Connor still remembered the look of horror as her snot-nosed, snivelling grandchild approached. She'd pleaded, 'Please don't tell your mother I forgot you – she'll kill me.' Of course, as any five-year-old would, he couldn't wait to blab all to his mum when she arrived from work to pick him up. There had been a furious row and after that his mum had had to make other after-school arrangements.

Even though he was young at the time, he could still recall his gran's deterioration. She began swearing a lot at first, which had been unlike her, followed by a loss of inhibition, taking to wandering around the house semi-naked. Her motor skills went, too. She became wobbly and unsteady on her feet, suffered weight and muscle loss, and had trouble swallowing. In the end she just faded away.

A few years back the family curse struck again, this time Connor's mum Annie began to show telltale signs of the disease.

She was now unsteady on her feet, but had good and bad days. Sometimes she was incredibly lucid when he called and at other times she had difficulty putting a sentence together.

Connor tried not to think of the future too much. There was a straight 50/50 chance he'd inherit the dodgy Huntington's genes. He'd been offered a test by his mum's consultant when he'd taken her for an appointment but had refused. What was the point? The disease was incurable, despite the encouraging noises scientists made every so often about a breakthrough.

It usually started to 'kick-in', as the consultant had put it, when those carrying the gene reached forty. Connor was now thirty-nine, so he guessed he'd learn soon enough. But he would, as the old adage had it, cross that bridge when he came to it. His philosophy was to live in the now, and right now his colleague needed all the help she could get.

In the last few weeks the Weasel had been feeling burnt out. The Seth murder had left him physically drained. He knew cocaine was damaging his body. He'd been doing so much of the white stuff that his septum was starting to wobble loose. But the Weasel felt it was worth the toll it had taken on his body. As the cocaine high began to kick in, he instantly felt better, and allowed himself the luxury of stroking his own ego.

The *Daily Herald* was at the top of its game and ahead of the pack because of *his* leadership. His misplaced self-belief would not even allow him to contemplate that the paper's success with the Seth murder had all been down to Connor and April's hard work and expertise. No, as far as he was concerned, he had ridden them hard to produce the goods, which they had done.

But now, 'the old dear had slipped up', meaning his plan to have her dismissed – without the need for an expensive payoff – and install his mistress in her place had just taken a massive step closer.

The news editor diced up another line of the white stuff and inhaled it deeply, flushed the toilet and walked onto the editorial floor. It had just gone 8 a.m. and the Weasel felt ready to take on the world.

27

A DEATHBED PROMISE

All three of Colin Harris's mobile phones were vibrating simultaneously. Since he'd 'put out the feelers' to find his sister's murderer, calls were coming in thick and fast from across Glasgow. Harris knew this wasn't out of loyalty or desire to curry favour with him. It was to do with the £100,000 bounty he had put on the head of his sister's killer.

He'd had to switch off the phones while visiting his mum's hospital bed. Old Jeannie had suffered a stroke a few days after April had interviewed her. Harris was no medical expert, but he knew his frail old mum wasn't long for this world. She looked tiny, with her skeletal body barely raising the starched hospital sheets. Her mind was scrambled from the massive aneurysm on the left-hand side of her brain, which had rendered the right-hand side of her body virtually useless.

But as Harris kissed her forehead to say his goodbyes, Old Jeannie's strength and lucidity suddenly returned. She gripped her son's hand tightly. Then with all her might she managed to spit out the slurred, but clearly audible words, 'Find him, son. Find Jackie's killer.'

Colin clasped his mum's bony fingers and promised, 'I'm working on it, Ma. Night and day I'm working on it.'

DCI Crosbie left the first session with Watt Wilson feeling invigorated. He had a spring in his step and a smile on his face for the first time in as long as he could remember. He could recall Watt hypnotising him with a silver medal dangling on a chain. Once under, he felt like a weight had been removed from his shoulders and all the restraints he had to show as a police officer vanished.

The detective had been able to pour his heart out, rhyming off the numerous frustrations from his professional career to his home life that had been building up inside him, like a big ball of fury, which would erupt with his foul-mouthed rants. He had sworn repeatedly and loudly under hypnosis, but he had enjoyed it. Watt Wilson had encouraged him to swear more and more. In fact, he recommended that every so often Crosbie should drive into the Campsie hills, that give Glasgow its unique skyline, and scream obscenities into the wilderness.

'That sounds like a fucking marvellous idea,' Crosbie had remarked, before Watt had ordered Crosbie to return his swearing alter ego back inside the deepest realms of his mind, like putting a 'genie back into a bottle'.

The detective felt good. He was ready to tackle his two murder cases with renewed drive and enthusiasm. And he didn't fear his inner self any more, even though it had threatened to derail his career. Instead, he had been actively encouraged to set it free. 'Like venting off steam,' Watt had explained, 'before you explode.'

'That old dear, April, was right – you are good,' he'd said to Watt as he left the hypnotist's home a happy man.

28

WEASEL WORDS

The Weasel had clearly been waiting for April to arrive. No sooner had she stepped foot on the *Daily Herald*'s editorial floor, he barked, 'You. HR. Now.'

By taking matters to human resources, the Weasel was making everything official. The unions had long been drummed out of the *Daily Herald*, and left toothless after the Thatcher government. New Labour had introduced new laws in the unions' favour, but the *Daily Herald*'s management steadfastly refused to negotiate with the likes of the National Union of Journalists. To appease the workers, and stay on the right side of the law, a staff association was formed instead. It was the elected members of this staff association who handled everything from pay negotiations to disciplinary actions. But since it was not funded by contributions from members' subscriptions, but by the owners of the *Daily Herald* itself, it was seen as little more than a company puppet.

It was an accusation that always annoyed the staff rep Davie Paterson. Davie was the former Father of the Chapel for the *Herald*'s National Union of Journalists branch. He was an old-school union type with the ruddy complexion of someone who enjoyed a right good drink. Paterson hated the new breed of managers like the Weasel, being of the firm belief that most problems could be sorted in the department, without official involvement from HR and the staff association.

Paterson looked flustered when he met April and Connor outside the HR department for the hastily arranged meeting, asking bluntly, 'What the fuck is this about, April? I only got summoned five minutes ago.'

Connor spoke on April's behalf. 'April's screwed up badly. She never called in after a story. The Weasel was waiting to splash what she'd got. They'd hung on all day waiting for her to check in. In the end they needed to get another splash – which I supplied.'

Another call from Colin Harris had taken care of that. Today's front page read:

HARRIS: I'LL PAY £100,000 TO CATCH MY SISTER'S KILLER
GANSTER'S BOUNTY BOOST

Davie Paterson sighed and softened his tone, 'April, old darling, you're too long in the tooth to screw up like that. What really happened?'

She'd never been the crying type. In fact, April hated how younger female colleagues would turn on the waterworks if things didn't go their way. But tears welled up in her eyes once more. She sobbed, 'My bottle went. I had a murder confession on tape which I knew was lies and so did the police. I was getting told to do one thing by the police and I knew I'd have to do the complete opposite for the paper. I just ceased to be able to make a rational decision. I think I've finally passed my sell-by date. This is a young man's game.'

'Don't talk pish,' Paterson barked. 'Can't have the toddlers taking over the creche. Then we'd really be in the shit. Right, this cunt is going to hit you with a gross misconduct charge. I want you to say nothing. Let me do the talking.'

Paterson burst through the door of the HR manager's office, clutching what looked like a caseload of notes. In actual fact they were just photocopies of the last staff association meeting's minutes, but it was one of the oldest tricks of the trade to look like you'd come to a fight armed to the teeth. Paterson was a short man – barely five feet five – but his presence filled the room. He sat directly opposite the Weasel and eyeballed him. For all his grand standing of being a tough nut, the fiery news editor could not meet Paterson's thousand-yard stare.

April took her seat next to Paterson and smiled meekly at the HR manager Patricia Sharpe, an unfriendly and stern type, whom April had learned over the years was Sharpe by name and nature.

Human resources – which had replaced the old-fashioned personnel office – was a growth industry as far as April could see. In the old days one or two strange little accountant types seemed to be able to handle the payroll and pension payments of an entire company with thousands of staff.

Now it appeared you needed a whole department full of strident, young go-getters with university degrees to do the same job. Of course, they'd argue that the job description had changed out of all recognition what with the ever-increasing number of EU employment laws, along with various company initiatives and benefits for staff. April suspected it was a ruse. HR workers were now some of the highest paid within newspapers, many of which were struggling to turn a profit.

Patricia Sharpe wouldn't have to bother her perfectly coiffured head with what stories she was bringing to the table today, unlike the reporters who were the very lifeblood of the industry. Yet a woman who'd never chapped the door of a murder victim's family was now sitting in authority over a time-served journalist like April. It just wasn't right.

Patricia opened the proceedings by saying, 'We are here because the company intends to start disciplinary procedure against April Lavender for gross misconduct.'

Davie cut her off mid-flow, growling, 'Aye, aye, we didn't think we'd come here for the fucking coffee, which is pish, by the way. Kenco this ain't.'

Patricia had had many meetings with Davie, and was expecting his usual gruffness. 'Now, David,' she responded using his Sunday name, 'you know I'm legally required to adhere to company procedure.'

'Legally what?' Davie snorted. 'This isn't *LA Law*, love. Just lay it on the table, what you've got and what this is really about.'

If Paterson had wanted to provoke a response, he certainly got it. 'I'll tell you what this is really about. *She*,' the Weasel said, aggressively pointing his finger towards April, 'didn't file yesterday when she was out on a splash story. She didn't even check in. And for that alone she has no place on my news team.'

Paterson's face turned red with fury, as he stared silently at the news editor, before exploding. 'First of all, if you point again at one of my members, you'll leave here with nine fingers – the other will be shoved up your arse. Secondly, *she* has a name. It's April Lavender, and she's had more splashes than you've had your hole, sonny. And thirdly, by saying she has no place on your news team, does that mean she's now sacked? If so, then why are we bothering our arses going through procedure when you've already acted as judge, jury and executioner?'

Patricia Sharpe interrupted, 'Right, that's enough. Please mind your language, David – and to answer your final point, no, April has not been dismissed. We want to establish what happened yesterday to see what, if any, disciplinary procedure should be followed.'

Paterson knew HR was backing down. He had won a concession. He then asked for what he had really hoped to gain from the meeting: 'I want an adjournment to be able to present our case of mitigating circumstances.'

Patricia instantly replied, 'Granted. We'll reconvene in two days' time. Until then April is suspended on full pay. Thank you both for your time.'

Patricia and the Weasel remained seated as Paterson led April outside.

When they were out of earshot, he stopped her and said, 'You have a stay of execution. Sort out in your head who you're working for – the *Daily Herald* or the Strathclyde polis. Then, when you've come to the correct conclusion, write your story. You'll find all is forgiven if you can produce an exclusive splash. Good luck.'

April was in floods of tears as she sat across from Connor in the Peccadillo café.

'Bastard,' Connor spat. 'What an utter bastard. I'd love to get someone like Colin Harris to take him out. Or better than that, I wish the Weasel would contract some horrible disease. Seriously though, why doesn't a back-stabbing bastard like him get terminal cancer instead of good people like Badger. Does that make me a nasty person?'

'Well, you can be pretty cutting with me, but nasty, no. I'd call you many things, but never nasty,' she answered truthfully. April had been about to give an 'oh, you don't really mean that' response and generally patronise her younger colleague, when she paused for a moment and thought about the hypothetical picture Connor had just painted.

Cancer was an awful, awful disease. She had nursed her own aunt and uncle through it until they were left with the skin hanging off their bones, stripped of all their dignity. Part of her wanted a self-obsessed loathsome individual like the Weasel to experience the same, to see him humbled and learn some humiliation, but experience had taught April only too well. There would always be another Weasel waiting in the wings, ready to take his place. 'And we thought our teachers were tough,' she laughed.

Puzzled, Connor asked, 'What the hell are you on about now, you daft old bat?'

She explained, 'Remember at school you always had a teacher you hated as you felt they were constantly on your case? Well, I couldn't wait to leave and be "free" from all that. School was a walk in the park compared to working life. I've had more bad bastard bosses than bad teachers. But to answer your question, no, Connor, I do not wish cancer on anyone. However, you reap what you sow. I know it's an age-old saying, but it's one I happen to believe in. We are good folk, with flaws like everyone else. Our saving grace is our flaws will never be as bad as the Weasel's.'

29

A NEW MAN

DCI Crosbie sat at his desk, looked at the mountain of paperwork and chuckled to himself. Before the session with Watt Wilson, his inner self would have been cursing profusely at the amount of work he had to get through. But the foul-mouthed fury within remained silent. That's why Crosbie could afford a smile. 'It worked. It actually worked. The old fraudster has cured me. In just one session – incredible.'

'Talking to yourself is not a sign of a sane mind,' Crosbie's senior officer DS Cruickshank said as he entered his office, taking Crosbie by surprise. 'Are you feeling alright? I'm worried the stress of the inquiry is getting to you.'

Crosbie leapt to his feet and chirped, 'I have literally never felt better, sir. And it's inquiries, sir – two of them. Selina Seth and Jackie McIvor.'

'Ah yes, the prossie,' Cruickshank snorted.

Crosbie deplored the way that society – including the police – never seemed to give a damn about streetwalkers. As far as Crosbie was concerned Selina Seth was the real prostitute. She didn't have to sleep with the various rich businessmen whom Crosbie's team were currently in the process of tracking down for questioning, but she did so. And willingly. Albeit not for fifty pounds a shag, but it had become clear from his inquiries that Selina definitely slept with men to help secure contracts for Seth International. In Crosbie's book that definitely made her a bigger 'whore' than poor Jackie who had simply slept with punters to feed her drug habit. From what Crosbie had learned, Jackie been a loyal and loving girlfriend before meeting the wrong man.

'Well, what's the update, Crosbie?' Cruickshank demanded.

'As you know, we covertly recorded an interview with Selina's husband Martin, after you obtained a warrant, sir, but it's thrown up more questions than answers, to be honest.'

'Like what?' Cruickshank said in an impatient tone.

'Well, like the way he claimed he'd strangled his wife,' Crosbie replied nervously.

'You mean to say that after I arranged to obtain a warrant to record Martin Seth, having to jump through hoops with a prickly judge to do so, you get a full confession yet don't bring the murder suspect in for questioning for one of the highest-profile murder cases the Strathclyde Force has had to handle in years? Am I actually hearing this correctly?'

Long, rambling, rhetorical questions were Cruickshank's speciality. But Crosbie stood his ground. 'Yes, sir. But he's lying, sir.'

'A hunch, DCI?' Cruickshank mocked.

'A fact, sir. We tracked his mobile phone signature to his parents' home at the time of Selina's death. We have collaborative alibis from his folks and his kids, including the six-year-old son. As you'll be aware, sir, a six-year-old is incapable of keeping a secret. Look at those weather balloon pranksters in America, sir.'

In 2009 a couple of reality TV wannabes staged the disappearance of their son, saying he'd been holding onto a weather balloon when it soared miles into the sky. The boy was later found, safe and well in their family home. When questioned by a TV crew, he immediately blurted out how his folks had told him to hide in the garage while they pretended he'd flown away.

The balloon analogy seemed to resonate with Cruickshank, as his tone audibly softened. 'Okay, so what next, Crosbie? The pressure I'm getting to solve this case is unbelievable.'

Crosbie explained the case so far. 'Forensics have several DNA samples from the crime scene. There's the usual contamination with DNA from a couple of police officers and a paramedic who were first on the scene, but two unidentified male samples, too. I also want to bring Seth in again. There are a few questions I'll make sure he's asked, that I'd like to hear his reaction to. Whoever did this, sir, we will get him.'

Cruickshank instructed Crosbie to keep him informed 'every step of the way' then turned on his heels and left.

DCI Crosbie smiled to himself again. 'I didn't even call him a cocksucker. I really am getting better.' He picked up his BlackBerry and called his new recruit – the formidable April Lavender.

30

BORROWED TROUSERS/ BORROWED TIME

April's mobile rang once more. She'd been ignoring most calls since her suspension, talking only occasionally to Connor. She hadn't even bothered telling her daughter what had happened. Jayne was always too busy with her own life to be concerned with her poor, old, mad mummy, April thought in a moment of self-pity.

April believed that, on the whole, she'd been a good mum. She would occasionally have to work late, and when a big story like the death of Princess Diana broke, she'd disappeared at short notice to the coastal town of Oban to try and interview Frances Shand Kydd, Princess Diana's mother. April had spent a week on Scotland's west coast not getting anywhere near Shand Kydd's front door, which was being protected round the clock by uniformed officers.

As she'd left in a hurry, she'd had to borrow a photographer's waterproof trousers, normally used by snappers at football games. She'd worn the plastic attire for three straight days, before she and some fellow female reporters had gone foraging into town for new clothes and knickers. There had been a real camaraderie between all the hacks on that job since it became apparent on the first day they wouldn't be getting any chats with the grieving mother. But since this was the biggest story in the world at the end of September 1997, they had all been ordered to stay put.

April's daughter had been seventeen at the time and had just started dating her first 'serious' boyfriend, which was a polite way of saying they were having sex. Maybe it had been a familiar look in her teenage daughter's eyes, but shortly before she lost her virginity, April had marched her down to the family doctor and insisted she was put on the Pill. Jayne was mortified, but April wouldn't take no for an answer, saying, 'You are not going to end up in the same shit as me. Pregnant, no job, no man – no way.'

But for one glorious late summer week, she got to escape all that. It was red wine and à la carte meals every night in the best restaurants Oban had to offer with the rest of the press pack. There had even been some time for a fling with one of the snappers. She'd never coughed to his identity, but he'd appreciated the return of his waterproof trousers with interest.

That all seemed so long ago now. When she looked in the mirror, an old woman stared back. An old woman who'd just suffered the indignity of being suspended from her job. But an old woman Connor had made promise not to give up. Together, he assured her, they'd find the truth.

DCI Crosbie's named flashed up on her mobile. This was one call she would not ignore today.

Connor arrived at Gartnavel's Beatson unit in a hurry. He'd received a distraught phone call from Badger's wife Rita, saying her husband didn't have long to live. As he approached Badger's bedside, he could see there had been some sort of incident. His wife was in tears and a medical team were wheeling away various pieces of equipment, with his old mentor clearly in distress.

Badger soon settled after a massive dose of morphine. He opened his eyes and stared at Connor. 'I thought that was me gone there, son. A heart attack, they reckon. A bit of a scare, to tell the truth. They zapped me with their doodahs there. That seemed to do the trick. But not long to go now, Connor. Not long at all.'

It was the first time in years Badger had used Connor's real name. He sat beside his mentor's bed, and without warning clasped Badger's hand, waited for the dying man to snatch it away and tell him to get lost. He didn't. Instead, the older man squeezed back.

Badger ordered his wife to, 'Go and get the boy a cuppa coffee, for god's sake – he must be gasping. I'm fed up with all your snivelling, anyway.' It was his way of telling his wife to take a break after the shock of seeing him nearly die before her eyes.

A nurse approached, and still Badger didn't let go of Connor's hand.

'How you doing, Nurse Ratchet?' Badger asked playfully.

'Now then, Mr Blackwood, you know very well my name is Miss McFarlane,' she responded.

'Aye, so you keep saying, but you're as sadistic as that Nurse Ratchet from *One Flew over the Cuckoo's Nest*, always poking and prodding me. Never giving a dying man a moment's peace.'

A dying man. Never a truer word spoken in jest, Connor thought. Badger was dying. This could be the last time Connor ever saw him.

'And who's your young friend?' Nurse McFarlane enquired with the hint of a twinkle in her eye. She was about Connor's age and attractive even in her unflattering striped tunic and shapeless blue trousers. Connor also noticed she wasn't wearing a ring on her wedding finger, although that was no guarantee she wasn't married, as many nurses in high dependency units removed all jewellery while on shift.

'You're in there, Elvis. This could be your Priscilla,' Badger beamed.

Both Connor and the nurse blushed slightly.

'I am not fourteen years old or whatever ridiculous age Priscilla was when she started dating Elvis,' Nurse McFarlane retorted.

'It's better if you just ignore him,' Connor interjected. 'That's what I always do.'

'Cheeky cunt,' Badger said in a mock sulk.

'Now don't make me get a swear box for you again, Mr Blackwood,' Nurse McFarlane said as she finished taking her patient's observations. She smiled briefly at Connor before leaving the two friends by themselves once more.

Badger nudged Connor. 'You're in there, lad. Gagging for it. I can tell. I'll get her number for you. Just leave it to your old man here – although I better make my move quick. I could be dead by teatime,' he laughed.

Connor thought to himself how no one would have known Badger had just had a heart attack and was riddled with cancer, as he sat in his deathbed teasing and joking while playing Cupid. Badger hadn't complained about his lot once. He'd accepted his fate with a bravery Connor doubted he'd ever have.

'Before I forget,' Badger said changing the subject, 'I've had loads of cunts coming up to see me. Sends Nurse Ratchet and her cronies mental. But I had a visit from plod – the CID boys, old-school, mind. Your man DCI Crosbie came up. My guys reckon he's a bit of a nutter. Caught the top brass's attention, and not in a good way. Watch yourself with that one, Elvis. A shifty bastard by all accounts.'

'They can talk,' Connor thought to himself. He'd met Badger's CID crowd and they were as shifty as they came. They were the sorts who thought nothing of planting evidence and beating up a few suspects every now and then.

He could imagine DCI Crosbie despising them with his morals and principles. In return, he would have made powerful, resentful enemies. They would go out of their way to soil his name as he kept ascending the career ladder. Connor didn't share his thoughts with old Badger, promising only to 'bear that in mind'.

Rita returned to the bedside with cups of coffee. She smiled at the sight of her husband still clasping Connor's hand. Badger had never been the emotional type, but it pleased her to see he was letting his tough guy facade slip, showing in his final moments the man she always knew him to be.

He finally let go of Connor to take his coffee. 'Thanks, Rita babes, proper coffee, too, clearly not from this dump,' Badger said a little too loudly, earning glances from the relatives of the three other patients in the ward.

'Right, you better be offski, sunshine. Don't give those cunts at work any ammo to get shot of you,' Badger ordered, not so subtly indicating visiting time was over.

Connor stood to hug Rita goodbye. He then negotiated the various tubes and wires to do the same with his mentor. 'You're simply the best, Badg,' Connor whispered in his mentor's ear.

'On your way, Elvis,' Badger said, this time with tears filling his eyes. 'On your way, lad.'

31

THE ONE THAT GOT AWAY

April and Connor sat in Crosbie's office telling the detective about April's suspension and how she feared her days at the paper were numbered. Connor said, 'So, you see, Detective, the *Daily Herald*'s Special Investigations unit has been split in half because of you – I think April will be putting in a claim for police compensation.'

Crosbie looked genuinely sorry about April's plight. He said, 'Would it help if I called this Weasel fella and explained that I put you in an impossible situation.'

'No, no,' April replied boldly, 'I'm a big enough girl to be able to look after myself. I've never allowed myself to be pushed around by any man – copper, editor or husband. I really don't know what happened to me yesterday. It's not like me to bury my head in the sand.'

Crosbie placed a hand on her shoulder and said quietly, 'We've all done it. A crisis of confidence. Sometimes I wake up in the morning and don't know who I am.'

April thought to herself, 'I bet you don't with that split personality.'

The detective changed the topic by studying a transcript of April's interview with Martin Seth once more. 'There's something missing here,' he said, 'and I don't know what it is.'

The three of them ran through various motives Martin might have for wanting his wife dead, from her numerous affairs to her constant over-spending and scant regard for the precarious financial situation her company found itself in.

'All of these are reasonable enough, but there's something else. Some other piece of the jigsaw which will link it all together,' Crosbie stated. 'I need you to interview Martin again,' he said directly to April. 'I need you to ask some other questions for me.'

Connor liked Crosbie the more he met him. He liked the fact that he had his detractors amongst the ranks. In many ways that meant he was doing his job properly and didn't need to resort to pinning everything on 'the local loony' as forces up and down the land were guilty of doing time and again. Even though he was seen as a new breed of high-flier in the force, in Connor's book he was an old-fashioned copper. He didn't leap to conclusions. He'd been as sceptical of Martin Seth's murder confession as April, even though it would have meant major Brownie points for both if they'd just taken Seth at his word. Connor saw a lot of himself in Crosbie. He was someone he not only admired but could easily see becoming a friend.

April agreed to do a second round of interviews with Seth, confident within herself that he was no killer.

Crosbie added, 'I was going to bring him in again myself. But he won't tell us anything under caution with his lawyer there. I have a hunch he may be ready to spill his guts to you though.'

Martin Seth looked like he'd come to the end of the line. He had visibly aged since April had seen him last, and had lost so much weight he looked deathly ill. He somehow seemed to have shrunk, too. His six feet two frame, now bent double, no longer filled the room.

'Where are the kids?' April asked, sparking a flicker of emotion in Martin's dead eyes.

He mumbled, 'With their nana and papa. It's better they stay with them. Safer. More secure. They'll be well looked after. Selina and I have some very decent life assurance policies, so we'll be leaving them a good chunk of change.'

April rummaged around in her bag for her tape recorder, as she could sense Martin was about to unburden himself. To confess. Maybe she'd even get the truth this time. He took no notice as she placed it on the coffee table between them, with its red light indicating it was recording. She then said softly, 'Go on, Martin. Get it off your chest. I know you didn't kill your wife. But I think you know who did.'

Connor waited down the private lane outside the Seths' home to allow April to interview Martin by herself. His car was concealed behind a hedgerow in a space used for turning on the narrow road. He got out for some fresh air. From his vantage point, he could make out part of the Seths' front gate.

Connor was just about to check his BlackBerry for emails when he caught a glimpse of a hooded figure darting to the Seths' entrance. He felt a surge of panic. He immediately dialled April's mobile as he dashed towards the gate. He was about to leap over the wrought-iron entrance when he was struck from behind.

Before his lights flickered out, Connor berated himself for thinking the intruder was working alone when it was clear he had back-up. His last thought before he passed out was of poor defenceless April. He felt his BlackBerry being prised out of his hand as his attacker pressed the disconnect button. It wouldn't have made any difference anyway as Connor's call had gone straight to voicemail. As a rule, April always switched off her mobile while interviewing people. She considered it bad manners to be interrupted by it.

But Martin Seth had his mobile on. It rang, playing a tinny-sounding version of 'Flower Of Scotland'. April remembered that Martin was a huge rugby fan. And all Scotland rugby support-ers loved the country's unofficial national anthem, especially the verse about sending the English King Edward's army home to think again.

'Look, I told you no,' Martin told his caller. 'What do you mean this is my last chance? What are you going to do? Kill me? Well, I've got news for you, buddy. I'm already dead.'

He hung up and stared at April offering no explanation. He then said sternly, 'You should go. Go now. It's not safe for you here.'

April knew the confessional moment had been lost, but she went for it anyway. Speaking in her softest tone and touching his wrist lightly she whispered, 'Tell me who killed her, Martin.'

He averted his eyes, pulled his hand away from hers, and said, 'She killed herself. She killed both of us. You should leave now. I have business to attend to.'

April packed away her notepad and recorder, and made her way to the door, pausing to try one last time, even though she knew it was futile. 'Are you sure you don't have anything you want to tell me, Martin?'

But his mind was elsewhere now. He gestured with his hand for her to leave, and she obeyed, showing herself out through the dimly lit hall and to the front door, which she noticed was slightly ajar.

April suddenly felt an animalistic fear, but just a fraction too late. A pair of rough hands grabbed her from behind, restraining her wrists, while a rag was stuffed into her mouth. She tried to grapple with her assailant, and stamped her high-heeled shoes, slamming them down on one of his big toes. 'Aargh, ya fucking bitch,' he moaned. But it was her last act of self-defence, as a builder's sack, made of tough white nylon, was pulled over her head to her waist. It was then bound tightly, and April felt two sets of large hands lift her up before throwing her onto what she suspected was the chaise-longue she'd spied in the hall.

'She weighs a fucking ton,' said one of her attackers.

'Aye, you could do with losing a few stone, missus,' the other one shouted in her direction.

They both had broad Glaswegian accents. But the fact they'd been joking amongst themselves meant April no longer felt she was in any great danger. She couldn't move, but she could breathe, and apart from being manhandled, she hadn't been hurt. Her attackers hadn't come for her. It was Martin they were after. She suddenly felt afraid for him.

She could hear doors opening and slamming shut all over the house as the assailants looked for Selina's husband. Heavy footsteps then thudded down the hall stairs and past April towards the front door. One of the men joked again, 'Try WeightWatchers, love, because that seafood diet you're on isnae working.'

'Aye, the see food and eat it diet,' the other quipped.

They were clearly a double act – but they had also failed to get their man. Martin had escaped. April began to wonder if she'd get that confession after all.

If only she could escape. 'It's alright,' she thought, 'Connor will be along soon.' Suddenly a feeling of dread swept over her. 'Oh my, I hope Connor's alright.'

Connor frantically untied the rope that bound the builder's bag.

He said, 'Without trying to offend, you look like a big sack of rubble. There's bits sticking out everywhere.'

April replied with a mumble, which sounded suspiciously like, 'Fuck you.' She was from Ruchazie, after all, one of Glasgow's rougher districts.

Connor took pictures with his BlackBerry, which made a fake shutter sound with every snap.

The sack moved around with a string of more mumbles.

'It's evidence, my dear, in case we need it. It's also a damn good story,' Connor added as he lifted the sack from April's body.

Even the hallway's dim light made her blink as she adjusted to her newly restored vision. She could also see Connor was in pain as he grimaced with every movement. The flash went again followed by the shutter sound. He clearly wasn't sore enough to stop taking pictures, she thought.

Connor looked at her sitting there, her ankles still bound with plastic ties and her mouth gagged with a cloth and gaffer tape. He said, 'Hey, you might finally lose some weight like this.' He took another photo for good measure, then with a deftness of hand, so April wouldn't expect it, he ripped the tape from her face.

April's eyes widened with the pain. She then spat the saliva-soaked rag from her mouth like a champagne cork from a bottle, and yelled, 'Owwwww!'

Connor inspected the sticky side of the tape, which was now covered with April's fine facial hairs, and laughed, 'Well, at least it's saved you getting your moustache waxed for a while.' He then sat down heavily on the chaise-longue beside his colleague and gingerly touched the back of his head.

April asked, 'Are you alright?' before wrinkling her nose and saying in an accusatory tone, 'Have you been drinking?'

Connor managed a half smile. 'I'll live – and I wish. About fifteen minutes after you went in, I saw someone leap over the gate and ran down to see who it was. But someone else was waiting for me, and all I remember was a whack to the back of the head before waking up slumped in the back seat of my car covered in booze. They'd doused me in whisky in the off chance I was discovered by cops or someone who would think I was just sleeping off a heavy night. Which makes me believe it was a pro who whacked me.'

April said, 'Well, the two goons who grabbed me were a right couple of gorillas. They wouldn't have been able to leap gazelle-like over any gates.'

A light came on in Connor's eyes as he said, 'Then it was the goons who carried me back to the car.'

They both said simultaneously, 'Harris.'

Connor continued, 'It was Colin Harris I saw leaping over the gate. He's small, wiry and athletic. He also doesn't go anywhere without his two heavyweights. The question is did they get what they were coming for?'

April said, 'I don't think so. The time they spent scuffling with me gave Martin the chance to escape. I guess he knew they were coming as he took a call just as I'm sure he was about to confess. He told the caller that there would be no deal and then ordered me to leave because it wouldn't be safe. I dragged my feet a bit just in case I could get that confession from him but the moment had gone. When I got to the front door I was jumped.'

Connor began tapping furiously on his BlackBerry sending the text, *Did u gt him?*

A few seconds later the BlackBerry's red light began to flash indicating Connor had received a message. It simply read, *No.*

He replied: *Betta luck nxt time. PS where did u gt a gag to fit April's big gub?*

Colin Harris texted back: *LOL.*

Connor showed April his reply.

She said, 'Did you know for years I thought LOL meant 'lots of love' instead of 'laugh out loud'. I used to get quite worried when I'd get texts or emails from guys in the office. Why don't people just write texts properly and grammatically correct. It would save a lot of misunderstanding in the world.'

Connor replied, 'LOM.'

With a quizzical look April said, 'LOM?'

He laughed. 'It's your new acronym – Lots Of Misunderstanding.'

'Now I've got a splash to file.'

32

DIM AND DENSER

April sat in the Tesco café at Craigmarloch near the Seths' family home. Connor had bought her a large tea, a roll and sausage covered in brown sauce with a Danish pastry to help her recover from her ordeal. He sat across from April and urged her to be quiet while he filed his copy.

April was amazed how Connor could write thousands of words from his tiny hand-held BlackBerry. She could barely read the screen unless she was wearing her extra thick reading glasses. As he sat watching him tap, tap tapping away at the miniature keyboard, she thought of how she'd learned to type at De'meers secretarial college, under the auspices of Miss Denser. She had spent a year there, all for the dubious honour of graduating from De'meers college as a Denser student.

Miss Denser was a Miss Jean Brodie type, an old spinster who looked as though she'd never cracked a smile in her life, never mind slept with a man. The school specialised in taking the dim-witted daughters of rich businessmen and teaching them secretarial basics, so that they could get a job in a large company and go on to marry other rich businessmen.

April had got in on a local authority bursary, the only one to do so in her class, and Miss Denser had made sure she knew it. She tried to make April feel as if she had no right to be mixing with the upper crust of society, or wealthy halfwits as April referred to them.

'Miss Tarte,' she'd bellow, for that was April's maiden name, one she'd been desperate to ditch for as long as she could remember, 'you've done it wrong again.'

A phrase that would follow April throughout her life.

'You've done it wrong again' could apply to her doomed

marriages and to her decidedly dodgy IT skills. Hardly a day went by without Connor shouting the same phrase across the broom cupboard office as she attempted to use the online archive or their desktop publishing system Hermes – nicknamed Herpes by long-suffering staff.

'You know they're talking of replacing Herpes,' Connor had casually mentioned one morning.

Any technological changes brought April out in a cold sweat. Whenever she felt she had mastered an operating system, and by mastered she meant she could successfully log on and limit her calls to the IT department to just a few per week, then the company would replace it.

Technology completely baffled her. She had no idea how the words Connor tapped into his BlackBerry would appear 'as if by magic', as she once let slip, in the following day's newspaper.

Connor had taken her by the arm and pointed to the sky and said, 'See that big silver bird? We call that an aeroplane. An aer-o-plane.'

After that she had kept her 'as if by magic' observations to herself.

Miss Denser aside, the truth was, she had actually enjoyed De'meers college as most of the girls were all right. April made friends with a couple of them. She had forgotten their names now, but she did enjoy taking Daddy's little princesses to rough pubs they would never have dreamt of frequenting, then laughing as they would get sozzled and snog the faces off apprentice trades-men instead of the rugby captains they were being groomed for.

But word of one of these little nightly excursions somehow slipped out and Miss Denser was furious. With a face like thun-der, she made an attempt to address the class but it was abun-dantly clear her poisonous words were directed solely at the young freckle-faced girl from the wrong side of town.

'I am told, from a very reliable source, that certain De'meers college students have been frequenting the Jacobite licensed prem-ises.' Miss Denser couldn't bring herself to use the word 'pub'. 'Let me make one thing absolutely clear,' she prattled on, 'the Jacobite is not an establishment fit for a student of De'meers college, to be seen laughing, joking and drinking with young men. Now I know some of you may not have a reputation to uphold, but De'meers college most certainly does. And young ladies from De'meers college are representing our fine school at all times.'

April could barely contain her tears of laughter. She loved the way Miss Denser saw no irony in the name De'meers college, but she simply couldn't help herself when she decided to play along. April piped up in the style of *Rumpole of the Bailey*, 'Miss Denser, these are very grave accusations, very grave indeed. I myself would never dream of entering such a tawdry establishment, but I have passed it once or twice and observed that there is frosted glass on all the windows and doors. So, I have come to the conclusion that your very reliable source, who allegedly witnessed students from De'meers college drinking and cavorting or whatever else – must have been inside the said Jacobite licensed premises at the time.' April finished triumphantly. 'Perhaps your reliable source could elaborate more and help us identify who these alleged students were?'

You could have cut the atmosphere with a knife as Miss Denser looked as if she was about to spontaneously combust. The other students could barely stifle their giggles as they sat eyes down and waited to see what on earth would unfold next.

Miss Denser marched to April's desk and stuck her index finger in her face. 'You, young lady,' she spat, 'are a bad egg.'

The truth was, Miss Denser had been rumbled by April. Every week she'd let down her tightly wound grey bun, swapped her matronly grey suit for more casual clothes, donned some make-up and headed to the Jacobite for some very large whiskies.

April and her friends wouldn't have recognised Miss Denser even if she'd joined their company. They certainly wouldn't have equated her with the ageing flirt at the bar pinching the backside of a married plumber.

April was wrong about Miss Denser on one account though. She had slept with a man – just about every regular in the Jacobite as it happened.

Connor snapped her out of her reverie. 'Copy all done and filed. Come on, let me drop you off at home.'

EXCLUSIVE by CONNOR PRESLEY

THE WIDOWER of murdered jewellery tycoon Selina Seth was in hiding last night after a failed kidnap attempt.

Martin Seth, 39, fled the family home in Dullatur, Cumbernauld, after three men broke into the £1.5 million mansion in a bid to abduct him.

Daily Herald crime reporter Connor Presley was attacked during the botched raid.

Connor, 39, was knocked unconscious by one of the assailants and a 58-year-old woman at the property – who refused to be identified – was bound and gagged.

Both were taken to hospital before being released.

Martin Seth's whereabouts is unknown.

It is believed a notorious crime lord was attempting to buy a share of Seth International – the multi-million pound company Martin co-owned with his late wife – even though the firm is said to be in financial difficulties since the brutal murder of Selina, 38, two weeks ago.

Last night DCI Crosbie said: 'We're keeping an open mind.'

33

PAYBACK

'Fifty-eight! Fifty-bloody-eight!' April remonstrated.

'Well, none of us is getting any younger, my dear,' Connor said, patronising his older colleague.

'I am fifty-six, you moron,' April seethed. 'I know it's a laugh to you, but management will look at the age fifty-eight in the paper and think, "Jeez, it really is time we got rid of old April. Look, she's pushing sixty. Time to put her out to pasture."'

'Should have been done years ago,' Connor coughed and muttered under his breath. 'Look, it's been a tough couple of weeks for you. You need to relax a little, you've aged terribly,' Connor added, clearly enjoying his little wind-up, 'and anyway, how do you know it was me? Maybe the subs changed it. Yeah, must have been the subs.' He laughed, using the age-old reporter's get-out clause.

'And I take it the Weasel made you take out my name?' she said.

'Yip, I argued like fuck for it. Glad to see many others in the newsroom did, too, but he said it was company policy while someone was suspended ... blah, blah, blah,' Connor explained.

The piercing ringtone of Presley's BlackBerry brought their conversation to a halt.

Someone other than April was not happy with the article. Colin Harris was attempting to keep his temper – and failing miserably. 'Connor, now everyone will think I murdered Selina. The fucking cops have been all over my pad this morning,' Harris roared down the phone.

'Consider it payback for the knock to my noggin,' Connor replied in an attempt to keep the conversation jovial.

'I may be a lot of things, but I don't go around murdering women,' Harris spat, getting angrier with every breath.

'I know that, Colin. And the cops know that, too. You're top dog around these parts, but you're not the law. You can't go around try-ing to kidnap legitimate business people who won't do deals with you or assaulting journalists just because you feel you can. You have to stick to dealing with scumbags. That's the natural order of things. The serious crime squad will see through any attempt by you to go legit. They'll shut you down, Colin. Repossess eve-rything. You'll be fighting them in court for years.' Connor con-cluded his lecture.

There was silence at the other end of the line until Harris whis-pered menacingly, 'Everything was going to plan before you blew it with these accusations.'

Connor sighed. 'Colin, think about it. You're a clever man and more streetwise than I'll ever be. Did you honestly think you could abduct the widower of the most famous murder victim in the land without it going unnoticed? It's the Icarus effect, Colin. You started flying too high and now the heat is melting your wax-wings. But you'll survive and bounce back, a bit like Lazarus. You always do. This is just a little glitch.'

'If you're finished with your ancient analogies, this is more than a little glitch. It's a fucking shit storm,' Harris said through gritted teeth.

Connor reluctantly admired the way Harris was well read. Despite leaving school unofficially at fourteen, he had made a point of reading many of the masters during his frequent bouts of incarceration, while his fellow inmates' literary scope stretched no further than that week's new wank mag.

'Colin, we've always been as honest as we can with each other, so I'm telling you straight: we have pictures of the cops raiding your house from this morning. Just to let you know.'

Harris swore under his breath before hanging up.

The photos looked great, thanks to DCI Crosbie waiting until there was enough light at daybreak for some decent shots by two *Daily Herald* snappers.

Unfortunately for Crosbie his alter ego hated early rises. He struggled to keep his inner monologue silent, attempting to cover up the odd 'cock suckers' and 'motherfucker' with a series of little coughs. But the rank-and-file officers were starting to gossip about their commanding officer being 'a bit of a nutter'.

Crosbie looked around Colin Harris's plush home. 'Tacky as fuck,' his inner self said out loud. Crosbie couldn't help but agree. From the white shagpile carpet to the white grand piano, a bit like John Lennon's in his iconic 'Imagine' video. Crosbie took a step closer to read a plaque on the piano lid. It wasn't like the Lennon piano – it *was* the Lennon piano.

'Fuck me,' Crosbie and his inner self said in unison.

'Did you say something, sir?' an officer behind him enquired.

'Yes, be careful with that piano. It'll make us a lot of money,' Crosbie ordered.

The detective was enforcing the Scottish government's Proceeds of Crime Act, introduced in 2002. It had proved to be a useful law enforcement tool as the police could seize the assets of known criminal gangs with the onus on the suspect to prove that their BMWs, giant plasma screen TVs and homes had been purchased with legitimate money. Since most of the criminals rarely paid tax it was usually an open-and-shut case.

But Colin Harris was no ordinary criminal. He insisted he had earned the bulk of his earnings from a series of bestselling books about his early crime career and claimed to have gone straight. In truth the paperbacks had sold a fraction of what Harris had said they had. However, it had allowed him to plough his profits from drug dealing into a series of legitimate businesses. His major problem was that his legitimate businesses grew at a much slower rate than his criminal enterprises, which is why he had been so keen to buy into Seth International. Although an ailing company in decline, thanks to its late co-owner's lavish lifestyle, it was still a household name, and it would have provided Harris with the perfect platform to launder his illegal money. If it had all gone to plan, it would have made him a very, very rich man.

Of course, the one thing many rich men fear is that some-one will one day take it all away. It was the only thought that truly worried Harris. The eventual outright acquisition of Seth International would have allowed him to sleep more soundly at night.

As John Lennon's piano was carefully wrapped and wheeled into the back of a Pickford's removal van, DCI Crosbie gave a wry smile. But his cheery mood soon disappeared as his other half made another appearance. 'You should have kept the piano for me, you stupid cunt – I play like Liberace.'

At around about the same time Colin Harris was being arrested by two detective sergeants on suspicion of attempted kidnap and assaulting two journalists. As he was read his rights and informed that anything he said may be taken down and used against him in a court of law, Harris muttered something under his breath. Even if the officers had heard him, they wouldn't have understood what Harris had meant as he quietly whispered, 'I owe you one, Elvis. I owe you big time.'

34

JIGSAW PIECES

'Okay, what have we learned so far?' Connor said as he began scribbling on a giant flipchart in the broom cupboard.

April grinned. 'Oh, this is exciting. It's like being in a lecture. Not that I ever went to university. I would've loved to have been a student. Cost me enough to put Jayne through university, mind you. Not that she ever seems in the least bit grateful.'

Connor interrupted, 'April, focus!'

'Sorry, sorry, I'm a terrible rambler. Please continue,' she beamed with a flash of her gold incisor tooth.

'I would never have known,' Connor sighed. 'Right. Selina Seth was brutally murdered by person or persons unknown. At the same time, we have a predatory, commuting serial killer on our hands. Coincidence? Or connected? Secondly, who would want to kill Selina?' His red felt-tip pen scribbled furiously. 'Martin Seth remains the prime suspect.'

'Ach, I don't know. I just don't think he's got it in him,' April interjected through a mouthful of biscuit.

'Your ample gut instinct aside,' he said, pointedly removing his packet of biscuits from the desk and locking them in a drawer, 'Martin Seth is still the main suspect. A crime so violent is usually one of passion. He's been her human punch bag for years, putting up with her drug-induced mood swings, her clamour for the limelight and her celebrity lifestyle, while he's left holding their business and family life together. My guess is he snapped. Maybe he followed his wife to that car park and saw her go down on god knows who. Whatever it was, Martin is in the frame. Then we have the prostitute Jackie McIvor, who unfortunately for the killer, was also the sister of Colin Harris, resident violent gangster of this parish. Harris is now hellbent on finding his sister's killer, and I have a funny feeling he'll beat the police to it. If that happens we'll never see the killer brought to justice.'

'Some might say justice will have been served,' April pondered.

'Maybe so, but god help us if we start turning to Harris and his type for their style of rough justice. You know he once burnt a man's genitals to a crisp with a blowtorch, only to later admit he'd tortured the wrong man … We can also throw Chantal into the mix. Selina's fake-tanned, boob-jobbed, drug-dealing, black-mailing former employee who was feeding her boss's drugs' habit directly from Harris.'

'How do you know it was Harris?' April enquired.

'He told me. We have a no-bullshit relationship – or at least we had. What he didn't tell me was why he stuck Chantal in it. It must've been Harris who told Selina her dog's body was skim-ming off five hundred pounds every week for herself. He probably leaned on her. Told Chantal not to talk to the press. But there had to be a reason. It wouldn't have made any difference to Harris, as he got paid either way. He obviously wanted something from Selina, and I think I know what.'

'Sex,' April said with a glint in her eye, unable to contain the excitement in her voice.

'No, I don't think so. He can get that on tap from Chantal and her like. He's a bad boy with money and power, and they seem to be an aphrodisiac to some women. I think Harris wanted in on Selina's jewellery business. What better way to launder his drug money, than through a high-profile, celebrity-led business? I bet he even used Chantal's blackmail case as leverage – possibly even encouraged the little trollop to threaten Selina. Then he could say to her, "If we were in business together, you wouldn't have to go through Chantal's type to get your gear."'

'Oooh, this is great fun. What else do we know?'

'Well, we don't know who killed the prostitute.'

'Couldn't the prostitute killer also have witnessed Selina's little tryst in the car park, then pounced when she returned to her car? I'm really getting into this detective stuff, I feel like Miss Marple.'

'Missing marbles more like. But you may be onto something. Maybe the serial killer was in that car park, but I don't think he killed Selina. Murderers like that don't tend to stray into different social groups. He's a prostitute killer. Someone like Selina is out of his league. Also he'd know that the cops' investigation into a prostitute murder wouldn't be of the same scale as that of a rich businesswoman like Selina. But I think you may be right. Maybe he was in that car park and witnessed Selina's real killer. So what would a lowlife like him do with that sort of information?'

April put her hand up as if she was in class. 'Oh, oh, I know this – go to the police.' She then berated herself before Connor had the chance. 'Sorry, no, that was stupid. He'd blackmail Selina's killer …'

'Maybe, Miss Marbles. That would mean Selina's real killer would have to be worth blackmailing. With knowledge brings power. If he hasn't already, I have a funny feeling that Martin Seth will meet our serial killer. I'd love to be there when he does.'

35

A HIGHLAND RETREAT

Martin Seth had fled to the Highlands to take refuge in the family's lodge. Now front-page news, the police, the press and his own family were all desperate to reach him, but they had little chance. He'd removed the battery from his phone and left it at home.

He'd headed north to Rothiemurchus and the place he called his refuge. The Seths had spent some of their happiest times there. As winter approached, there was a permanent nip in the clean air, and the lodge offered a breathtaking view of the Cairngorms, whose rounded black peaks looked like a school of humpback whales.

Martin loved the area for its miles of cycle tracks, which had taken the family on many adventures. Sometimes they would stop for a picnic by a stream on the sprawling Rothiemurchus estate or take a break in the Glenmore café, a rickety wooden affair on stilts, decorated with old postcards and skiing posters, where their children would shriek with excitement as the red squirrels, finches and occasional pine marten came down to the deck to feed on the ready supply of nuts.

But best of all, it was in this romantic heart of the Highlands where Martin had felt close again to his wife. He had been besotted by Selina the moment he saw the tall, confident blonde at high school. She could have had the pick of the best-looking boys in her year, but for some reason she choose him. From that moment on, no matter how badly she treated him, he had always felt lucky that she'd chosen him.

They fell in love together, although he always knew he loved her more than she loved him. They had lost their virginity with each other, and they became unplanned parents when Selina fell pregnant at just seventeen years old. This had not been part of her master plan. She refused to be yet another young, single mum from a Glasgow housing estate. Selina made sure that Martin quickly proposed before booking the first available date at the registry office. She would later claim she became pregnant on their short honeymoon then lie that the baby had arrived early.

Selina had greatly resented being home alone with the child while Martin had scraped a living at the family garage. 'This is not our future, Martin,' she had once berated him. 'I'm not going to stay at home cooking all day and changing shitty nappies as you work all hours for a crappy twelve grand – no way.'

Selina was stretching the truth as usual. She was a terrible cook and barely knew how to turn on their cooker. Martin prepared most of the meals when he eventually got home shattered from fixing cars. As for changing nappies, he couldn't recall how many times he'd walked through the front door to find a full nappy hanging off their toddler, while Selina sipped white wine and flicked through the latest celebrity gossip magazine. But, to her eternal credit, she did come up with a lucrative business idea, after studying the jewellery worn by the stars in her beloved mags.

At first she unashamedly ripped off the designs, making her own copies on a DIY jewellery set at home. Her first efforts instantly sold out to her friends, who read all the same trashy mags and envied the same celebs as Selina. Then she advertised the designs online with the promise that you could 'wear the same jewellery as the stars for a fraction of the price'.

Selina was doing such a roaring trade making the jewellery at home she found looking after their toddler a major inconvenience. The baby was despatched to a childminder by day as Selina started working round the clock. By her third month of trading she had made Martin's annual salary and ordered him to quit the garage to help her.

Things were going well, until one of the major jewellery designers spotted the Seths' cheap rip-offs on the net and threatened serious legal action. Selina quickly closed down the site and decided to go legit. She had always been a quick learner and soon came up with her own designs. Martin found his own role making everything tick behind the scenes, but it was his wife's ambitious streak which continued to give the company momentum.

Even falling pregnant again hadn't slowed her down. Martin only prayed the second child was his, knowing full well his wife had started playing away from home.

Soon television came calling. Selina was an ideal candidate for the daytime shows, as a successful businesswoman, wife and hard-working mother. The truth was, a nanny and grandparents now raised their children and there wasn't a week that went by when she wasn't in the arms of some man who wasn't her husband.

Just the thought of his wife kissing another man brought Martin out in a cold sweat. But here, at their lodge, with its spa pool on the wooden decking, its walls decorated with antlers from the estate's reindeer herds, and its woodburning stove, there were no other men. Just the love they had once shared together as a family.

Martin stood in the empty, dusty lounge and wept for the past, when his children still had a mother and he still had a wife.

The only person to witness Martin's distress was Osiris, standing in the fading autumnal light outside the lodge, enjoying the misery that was unfolding within. The killer had found it easy to pursue Martin, after he had seen him fleeing from his family home to head north. He smiled to himself. 'Your day is about to get a whole lot worse.'

36

COOL CUSTOMER

Colin Harris could be charm personified when he chose to be. Today was not one of those days. He sat alone in the interview room at Strathclyde Police headquarters waiting for DCI Crosbie. One of the overhead fluorescent lights flickered intermittently. Harris had never thought of himself as being photo-sensitive, but the strobe-like effect was making him feel physically sick.

Crosbie stood outside the interview room quietly chuckling to himself as he watched Harris's obvious discomfort through the one-way observation hatch. He loved how even the hardest criminal would be left squirming under the faulty bulb's insanely annoying flicker. 'Who needs waterboarding when a dodgy light will do,' he thought. 'Time we went in and put Mr Harris out of his misery.'

'Good morning, Colin,' Crosbie said cheerfully.

'It's Mr Harris to you, where's my lawyer and sort out that fucking light?' Colin demanded.

'Your lawyer is on the way and, oh, has that bloody light gone again? It'll take me three memos before maintenance are dispatched – I may as well break a few Health and Safety rules and do it myself.' As he climbed onto a chair beneath the offending light, Crosbie said, 'That reminds me of that old joke, "How many policemen does it take to change a lightbulb? None – it turned itself in."' Crosbie laughed just a little too heartily at his own joke, before placing the fluorescent tube on the table and taking the seat opposite Harris.

'Don't mind if I wait here until your lawyer gets here, do you?' Crosbie asked, not really caring what the answer would be. He was staying put.

'My lawyer is going to free me and get all the stuff you've nicked back. And your plods better not have scratched my Ferrari,' spat Harris.

Crosbie chuckled to himself again, infuriating Harris even further. Truth was, the gangster's £250,000 sports car was sitting in Crosbie's parking space outside. He planned to drive it himself until he was told otherwise by his superiors.

He could feel his inner self take over when he looked Harris straight in the eye and said, 'The thing is, Colin, I don't give a fuck what you do to journalists. Like taxmen they serve a purpose but it doesn't mean we have to like them.' Crosbie could hear the words tumbling from his mouth but knew he was powerless to intervene. The DCI's 'dark side' continued: 'But I do have a problem with you trying to muscle in on a dead woman's business. What an arrogant prick you really are.'

Harris opened his mouth to protest then thought better of it.

'To think you could lean on Martin Seth when his wife is at the centre of a major murder inquiry. Well, this shit storm I've brewed up for you is a little reminder, Colin, that you don't operate above the law. I can fuck with you whenever I like. And I like it, Colin. I like it a lot because I am a bad motherfucker.'

Harris knew a fellow psycho when he saw one. He wasn't scared – he never was – but he also knew just how unpredictable they could be.

There was a knock at the door.

Before Crosbie got up to let the lawyer in, Harris stared at the detective and said, 'That may be so, but I'll still catch my sister's killer before you do.'

AN UNEXPECTED GUEST

'Hello,' Osiris said without emotion, as Martin opened the lodge door to him. 'We need to talk.'

Martin said nothing and calmly closed the door behind the killer. It was almost as if he'd been expecting this moment. 'Tea? Coffee? Something stronger?' he asked his uninvited guest.

Osiris stood casually by the woodburning stove, an elbow on the old railway sleeper that had been converted into a mantelpiece. His right hand was thrust deep inside his waterproof jacket. He stood poker straight. His thin build and posture made him look taller than his five foot eight frame. He never once took his eyes off Martin, who was slumped exhausted in the couch facing him.

Osiris wasn't an emotional being, certainly not in the conventional sense at least. He had feelings, but for all the wrong things. He loved being in control, having the power to manipulate people and their circumstances. He thrived on having the choice over life and death, but he had a use for the broken shell of a man who sat before him, who barely had the energy to make eye contact.

Martin would either agree to his proposals or die right here tonight in the lodge. As far as Osiris was concerned, it was a no-brainer. He hoped Martin wouldn't force him to kill him, but he had a feeling Seth might choose death as the easier option.

THE PUSSY CAT

April was exhausted. Everything from being bundled into a builder's sack to her suspension was beginning to take its toll. But it was the thinking, the constant whirring of her brain as she tried to work out who did what and what to do next that really drained her. She often wondered what it would be like to have a simple job like a shelf-stacker where she wouldn't have to engage her brain.

April had once made the mistake of expressing this to Connor, who had snapped back, 'Working in Asda wouldn't have bought you your big house.' Of course, he was right.

Whenever she was feeling down she would visit her rich friend Flo, who lived in Bearsden, one of Glasgow's more salubrious suburbs. Like April, Flo had been married and divorced a number of times, too. Her last one hadn't been a total disaster though. Her husband owned a substantial steel company and had cheated on her with his secretary. Unfortunately for the wayward husband, new divorce laws had seen partners entitled to not only fifty per cent of previous earnings, but of future earnings, too.

Flo's £17 million divorce settlement had set a Scottish record. As she had said to her ex as they left court, 'Your secretary was one expensive fuck. I hope she was worth it.'

Since then Austrian-born Flo had turned into a Cougar – a mature, rich woman who pursued younger men. She had loved the freedom her independent wealth had brought her and enjoyed clubbing and having sex with men who were often younger than her sons. As she had once said to April, 'I don't feel guilty at all, darling. Men have been screwing woman half their ages since time began. It's time we caught up.'

Flo looked fabulous. She had an air of someone with money. She was slim, trim and toned from gruelling sessions with her

personal fitness trainer – 'Both in and out of the gym, darling.'
She had new breasts and even a 'designer vagina' she had once
shown April with pride.

April had never thought front bottoms were particular attractive, her own especially, but she couldn't help but admire Flo's.
'That is one perfect pussy,' April had observed before they dis-
solved into fits of laughter.

Although their lives were now worlds apart, the pair had
remained firm friends for over thirty years.

As Flo opened a second bottle of chilled Chablis, April poured
her heart out about work, being suspended and then bound and
gagged.

'Oh, I knew I had something to tell you, darling,' Flo suddenly
remembered. 'Selina was screwing your boss.'

'What!' April spluttered.

'Ya, your editor. Fair hair, side parting, slippery sort – married,
of course, can't remember his name, such an inconsequential man.'

'Nigel Bent?'

'Ya, that's him.'

'Flo, are you *absolutely* sure? This is serious.' April was back in
professional mode.

'Yes, darling. I met them at some function. They were trying
their damnedest to ignore each other so people wouldn't suspect,
but he couldn't take his eyes off her. I think the poor man was in
love. I was sitting next to Selina. She'd drunk a fair bit and she told
me. She was like that, you know, very boastful. Frankly, I didn't see
much to boast about. But, as we all know, love is blind.'

April took a while to digest all this information – she knew it
was dynamite. 'I need more drink, more nibbles, Flo. Come on,
make with the nibbles. I need brain food,' she demanded.

'Oh, you're such a glutton, my chubby little darling. But I do
love you,' Flo grinned as she headed to the kitchen. She always
made sure she was well stocked when April came to visit.

39

THE ANGEL OF DEATH

Wanting to die is a very strange feeling. Martin didn't want to share his suicidal feelings with anyone because he knew what their advice would be: see your doctor, get a course of antidepressants, talk about it with a counsellor. Martin wanted none of these things. The thought of taking 'happy pills' just depressed him more and he was never the 'Let's get your feelings out in the open' type either.

It wasn't a cry for help. Martin really did want to die. He was a shell of a human being. Where there had once been love, hope, ambition, excitement, there was now nothing but apathy and failure. He had failed hopelessly at being a husband. He had failed to fight to save his marriage, allowing his wife to come and go as she please with whomever she wanted.

He'd often wondered how it had all come to this. They had once been so in love. Now he was a widower he couldn't even face up to being a parent and all the duties that went with it. He didn't want to think about his kids, painfully aware that he planned to leave them orphaned.

But he could feel Osiris's eyes boring into him and somehow felt the stranger was looking directly into his soul.

'I know who killed your wife. I saw him with my own eyes,' Osiris said, staring straight at Martin.

Martin momentarily lost his dead-eyed look. There had been a flicker of light as his old confident self tried to resurface. Osiris knew he was taking a gamble, but he'd calculated it was worth it. His self-help guru had encouraged him to make a 'life plan'. He could hear the whining American voice say, 'If you don't know what you want in life, then how the hell will anyone else?'

How ironic, he thought, that he was now using these mantras

for evil. But with a steady income from Seth International for professional services rendered for the revenge killing of Selina's murderer, Osiris would be free to roam and kill around the country at will. He would no longer need to lead his double life as a transport manager by day and serial killer by night.

And if Martin said no? He'd hang him from the rafters of this very chalet, as who in their right mind would think it was anything other than the suicide of a guilty man. 'So, what's it going to be, Martin? Stick or twist?' Osiris felt a little corny trotting out such a phrase but it seemed to fit the moment. 'Are we going into business? You, the widowed entrepreneur. Me, the silent partner. Or silent assassin if you like.'

But Martin's eyes had returned to their trance-like state. The man simply wasn't capable of bouncing back off the ropes. In Osiris's dark heart he realised the man who stood before him must truly have loved Selina, even though Osiris had seen for himself the slut she really was.

He gently placed the noose over Martin's head. The widower didn't even flinch, almost welcoming the actions of his angel of death. This would most definitely be a mercy killing. But, all the same, Osiris would still enjoy watching him die.

Out of all the hundreds of erroneous pieces of information Colin Harris had received, he finally took the call he had been waiting for.

'Are you sure?' he said, trying to contain the excitement rising in his voice. 'Where was it and what did he look like?' Colin jotted down the details. 'And the car? I need to know what he was driving.' His face fell. 'What d'you mean you can't remember what type of car it was? Come on, think. You must recall something about it.' A smile slowly crept across the face of one of Glasgow's most feared gangsters. 'Yeah, I guess that'll do instead,' he said, chuckling to himself as he wrote down the full licence plate number the caller had memorised. The tip-off would cost him £100,000 if it led to his sister's killer, but for Harris to have his revenge it would be worth every penny.

The money he spent keeping one of Scotland's leading lawyers on a retainer was also worth its weight in gold. He was out on bail after being charged with the attempted kidnap of Martin Seth. It meant Colin Harris was once again a free man. But now he was angry. And when he was angry, he was even more dangerous.

40

AN INDECENT PROPOSAL

April had just enjoyed a long, leisurely lunch at Risotto, an easygoing Italian restaurant where she often spent entire Sunday afternoons. Sometimes she would take Jayne, but they would usually end up bickering. Therefore, if she truly wanted to relax, eat and read the *Sunday Times* over a bottle of wine, then she went to Risotto alone.

April knew the owner Luigi well. Sadly, Luigi's wife had died six months ago from cancer. April had lent a sympathetic ear on her regular weekend visits, hearing in minute detail how the aggressive form of lung cancer she'd contracted had rampaged through her body. She could always connect with other people's sorrow, as she had suffered too with the loss of the child she never, ever talked about to anyone. That's what made her writing so heartfelt.

Luigi pulled up a chair and sat down next to April. He had aged terribly over the last year as his beloved Maria had fought in vain against the disease. He now had sad, baggy eyes. The twinkle had long gone out of them. 'Aw, April,' he sighed, 'Am-a feeling right sorry for masel, so am are.'

Luigi's accent was a curious mix of strong Napoli Italian and broad Glaswegian. Sometimes he'd switch between the two mid-sentence.

April put a consoling hand on his knee and said, 'I know, Luigi. You'll never forget Maria, but it will get better. And she would hate to see her Luigi so depressed.'

He managed a half smile. 'You're right. She'd say to me, "Hey, Luigi, your-a face is scaring all the customers away – now cheer-a up-a."' He changed the subject. 'Now, April, tell-a me. How is the hunt-a going for this-a mad-a-man you are writing about in the news-a-paper?'

April actually hated talking about stories in her time off – more so now she was suspended from duty. She was an old-school journalist in that when something was written and filed, it was instantly forgotten about. She didn't even like recalling stories for people socially. All the detail had gone into her copy, and she actually couldn't recall most of it, even if she'd wanted.

On more than one occasion April would take a call from someone and it would be clear that she didn't have a clue who they were. When they explained they were the subject of April's centre spread that day, the penny would finally drop. 'Oh yes,' she would lie, 'of course. I know who you are.'

The fact was, April had written the story a week before it made the paper and it was long gone from her mind.

Luigi continued, 'I may-a have-a some-a news for you. My cousin visits the red-a light-a district. He likes-a the whores. He's an arsehole. But he-a saw something one-a night that might be useful to you. He cannae go to the cops, of course. His-a wife would a kill him. And no bloody wonder.'

Luigi told April that his randy cousin had witnessed a prostitute being attacked in a car then dumped in the street. It was important enough for April to fish out a dog-eared notepad from her handbag and jot down some shorthand.

'That's very interesting. Very interesting, indeed,' April told him truthfully.

'It's-a even better, my dear. He has this …' Luigi showed April his mobile phone. After rooting around in her handbag she eventually found her reading glasses and could see the image he was trying to show her.

The information which had cost the ruthless gangster Colin Harris £100,000 April had just got for free.

'There's-a something else, April,' Luigi said, suddenly looking sheepish. 'Will you marry me?'

It had barely gone nine o'clock on Monday morning when Connor received his first text message of the day: *B R N jst a month. Tel Marvel 2 gt back on on ;)*. He loved trying to decipher April's text messages. They were a typical mix of abbreviations and emoticons, some of which he was convinced were just typos, but what made them so unique was that April had been unable to switch off her mobile's predictive text option. Unfortunately, there was no software, however advanced, that could predict what April was thinking.

Connor had got pretty adapt at working them out all the same.

B R N jst a month. 'Easy,' he thought to himself, 'Be there in just a mo,' as the predictive text always turned mo into 'month.'

Tell Marvel 2 get back on on ;). Well, since they had arranged to meet in the Peccadillo, Marvel would be the waitress Martel. And the *back on on* had to be 'the bacon on'.

Some folk had their crosswords or their Suduko. Connor had April's texts. The Enigma code breakers at Bletchley Park could not have done better.

He texted her back in plain old-fashioned English: *Try to be a bit quicker than a month, you BOC (that's Batty Old Cow), and I'm sure MARTEL already has the bacon on.*

April was soon tucking into a Peccadillo breakfast special. Connor opted for a simple bowl of muesli.

He studied her with a wry smile as she told all about Luigi's unexpected marriage proposal in between great mouthfuls of food. Connor fully expected her to die this way, inhaling a whole link sausage during a long, inane explanation about hanging baskets or whatever else had happened to her that weekend. Like a pensioner having a heart attack on a golf course, at least she'd pass away doing what she enjoyed the most.

Suddenly, Connor's mind clicked into focus, and it had nothing to do with the lecherous old Italian trying to get his end away. 'Did you say Luigi's cousin might have seen our killer?'

'Oh yes, I almost forgot, after he got me all flustered with asking for my hand.' April rooted around in her handbag, 'Here it is,' she announced, producing the old notepad and studiously flicking through the pages. 'A red Ford Mondeo. And its licence plate.'

'Are you sure, April? Are you sure that's the number plate?' Connor asked emphatically.

'Oh yes, look,' April said, shoving her mobile phone in his face. There was a grainy picture of a Red Mondeo, with its fuzzy number plate. 'Bluetooth,' she announced triumphantly, 'Jayne showed me how to switch it on and Luigi just transferred his cousin's photo to my phone.'

'Wonders will never cease,' Connor said with a touch of pride. 'You may be a BOC but you always come up trumps.' He kissed her affectionately on the forehead.

'Luigi kissed me there as well, but the dirty old bastard also managed to cop a feel of my tits, too.'

'Who said romance was dead?' Connor grinned.

Colin Harris was also having bacon for breakfast. He had tucked a linen napkin into his collar to prevent any grease dripping onto his expensive Gucci suit.

He was no stranger to fine wining and dining. Glasgow's famous seafood restaurant Rogano's, nestled between Royal Exchange Square and Buchanan Street, could always find a table for Colin Harris even at their busiest times. In fact, he'd worked there on his bestselling autobiography, *A Matter of Life and Death, with his biographer Big Mac.* But this morning it was in the dank basement under the floorboards of the Portman bar that Colin found himself, dictating to three monstrous men who sat around the scruffy wooden table, lifeless pints of Tennent's lager in their massive hands even at this early hour.

Harris said, 'We know the number plate was false' – the gangster had discovered that information illegally from a 'contact' who had access to the vast database at the DVLA in Swansea – 'but that doesn't matter as we know the car and have an accurate description of our man. Now we've got to have our peelers out everywhere to catch him. He will surface again, twats like that are incapable of lying low, and when he does, I want him alive. Understand? No one is to touch him until I get there.'

Harris gave each of the three goons a bulging envelope, adding, 'That's five grand each, another five when you nail him.'

Tracking down Osiris had cost Harris heavily so far, what with the reward money he had to pay his informant, the £10,000 each for his heavies, and the £5,000 sweetener for his DVLA mole. But he would have paid ten times that to catch his sister's killer.

'Happy hunting, guys,' Harris said with a sadistic grin as the monstrous men headed for the steep steps that led from the basement to a trap door behind the Portman's bar.

None of the regulars batted an eyelid as the three gorillas squeezed themselves through the narrow service hatch and headed for the exit. The same way the regulars never saw a thing when the heavies would occasionally bundle a stranger through the same trap door to the hell that lay beneath.

41

A NEW RECRUIT

DCI Crosbie was now working on a triple murder inquiry. He knew every detail of the deaths of Selina Seth and the prostitute Jackie McIvor, but this morning he was staring at a new autopsy report – for Martin Seth.

Martin's death fell under the jurisdiction of the Northern Constabulary, since his body had been discovered at the Seths' family lodge near Aviemore, but as Martin had been the prime suspect in the murder of his wife, Crosbie had been asked to work with his Highland colleagues on the case.

In the usual non-emotional and clumsy writing style of the head pathologist, the autopsy papers detailed how Martin had been killed: 'Death by restriction of the airway caused by hanging. But it is the view of this pathologist that the euthanasia had been staged as the overturned chair was a foot too short for the height required for the deceased to place his head through the noose, meaning he either expertly jumped from the chair, placing his head in the noose, then was able to tighten it mid-air – which is theoretically possible – or that his head was placed in the noose at ground level and he was hoisted by assailant(s) unknown into a hanging position.'

Crosbie smiled to himself. 'Typical pathologist, always covering their arses. Of course it's "theoretically possible". It's theoretically possible I could shag Claudia Schiffer but it ain't going to fucking happen.'

So, someone killed Selina Seth. Someone else murdered Jackie McIvor. Colin Harris tried to either kidnap or blackmail Martin Seth – or both – and now Martin was dead.

DS Cruickshank burst into the room. 'Any leads, Crosbie? Anything at all? Or will we wait until the killer keeps on killing until we catch the fucker red-handed? What the fuck is going on, Crosbie? What the fucking hell is going on?'

Crosbie had never heard Cruickshank swear before. He feared it would spark off a response off the Richter scale from his inner self, however, he remained eerily calm and in a measured, assured tone, replied, 'Just one more day, sir, and I'll know where we're going and start making arrests. I need just one more day.' This statement was said more in hope than anything. Now he desperately needed to hire an ageing new recruit.

The staff rep Davie Paterson was as gruff as usual when he called April. 'How you getting on, old yin? Got your head screwed back on yet?'

April sighed but didn't give much away. 'Yeah, hanging in there, thanks.'

Paterson lowered his voice as if making a confession. 'Look, I've been asking about, to get a feel for what the company really want from this whole disciplinary nonsense, and it's not looking good, April. They want you out.' He let the phrase hang there, to allow it time to sink in, before continuing, 'It looks like you've made an enemy of the Weasel, and Bent has no intention of calling off his Rottweiler. You're screwed, my dear, unless you have a joker up your sleeve. If not, then it's a case of getting as much out of them as possible. They're trying to wriggle out of giving you the full amount, with this gross misconduct rap. But that won't stand up in a tribunal when you say they put you under undue pressure. By my calculations you've been here twenty-five years. You're due a month for every year's service, plus your three months' service and anything else we can try to lob in. You should be walking out that door with about two and a half years' wages, but these two cunts just aren't playing ball. They want to sack you. We could claim anything from sexual harassment to age discrimination. No hang on, you're mad as fuck, right? Have you ever had that properly checked out? If a kind doctor would go on record to say you have early-onset Alzheimer's, then that would go down as a disability. And if they discriminated against a disabled person then, Jeez, April, the sky's the fucking limit. Screw the thirty-one months' pay-off, we could be looking at three years. That'll give you a nice little retirement pot, eh?'

April broke into her customary throaty laugh, thanked Davie for his help and encouragement and hung up. She then dried her eyes and cheeks of the tears that had been streaming down her face. He'd hit a nerve. Early-onset Alzheimer's was a fear she lived with every day. Both her folks had suffered with it. They had not only forgotten each other's names, but even the fact that each other had even existed. When they were put into separate nursing homes, both would regularly be found in other patients' beds, thinking that was their partner.

Connor called a few minutes later, sending April off on one again. She sobbed how she feared she'd end up like her parents. But if she expected to hear sympathetic words down the line then she should have known better. Instead, Connor chuckled then said, 'Ach, what are you worried about? You'd be none the wiser. And anyway, think of it like this – with Alzheimer's, every day would be like an adventure with all those new people to meet. It wouldn't be any different from how you are now – you can't remember anything from the day before anyway.'

Connor made April laugh. She appreciated his easy ability to put life into perspective. She'd always been a mad old bat. Last week she'd even forgotten it was Jayne's birthday, which had led to a week of frostiness. When her daughter finally confronted April about her forgetfulness, she'd laughed it off as not being important because 'it's only your twenty-ninth birthday anyway', only to be informed that it had actually been her milestone thirtieth.

'Right, have you stopped all this self-pity pish?' Connor said, 'Because we have work to do.'

Connor had also made a call to a contact who had instant access to the DVLA computer and asked him to run a check on the registration number April had got via Luigi's kerb-crawling cousin. Ironically, it was the same 'mole' who had charged Harris £5,000. But it would cost the reporter next to nothing, except perhaps a few pints in the pub, as his contact was also his cousin Robert.

Robert said, 'It's a false plate, Elvis, but listen, someone else called in that exact number, too.'

Connor now knew for certain he was on the right track. Getting caught acquiring the services of a prostitute wasn't nearly as serious as driving around with a fake set of number plates. Obtaining fake plates was far more difficult these days since new government regulation meant you had to produce a vehicle registration form along with proof of identity and address. That meant the driver of the red Mondeo had probably had his false plate – or several plates – made up for a while. It also meant he was a professional. The fact that Colin Harris was on the case too only confirmed it.

Connor could do one of two things. He could tell the Weasel and his editor Bent everything he knew. They would then splash something along the lines of 'THE RED MONDEO SUSPECT' and every unfortunate middle-aged man driving a red Ford would be pulled by the police or open to vigilante attacks. Or, he could use the information to actually catch the bastard. Connor chose the latter.

He could not mobilise the same number of street contacts as quickly and as efficiently as the gangster but he could get access to the city's extensive CCTV network via DCI Crosbie.

Now he knew the make, model and colour of the car he was after, even if the killer changed the fake plates again, they would still be able to nail him, and quickly. But he needed bait. He knew the killer was not particularly fussy. If it was the same man who had been carrying out attacks over the years then he had targeted the young, old, skinny and fat. Dominating his victims and inflicting fear and pain were the name of his game.

Connor knew a woman who had the guts and wherewithal to act as bait. A very big piece of bait to catch a ferocious predator. He phoned April again. 'Sorry to interrupt you while you're no doubt eating, but I need you to be a streetwalker for the night.'

'Sure,' April said without pause, 'maybe I'll bump into Luigi's cousin, the dirty bastard.'

'Hmmm,' DCI Crosbie pondered out loud, 'I hope you know, you'll be taking one big tit fucking risk.'

'Well put,' April smiled.

Crosbie ignored her, letting his foul mouthed stream of consciousness continue, 'It's just a twating hunch, but I think Connor could be right that our prostitute killer prefers older streetwalkers. Jackie McIvor was just a murder of convenience. There have been many older sex workers killed or badly assaulted down south over the years. Some have been linked, most haven't, but I've got a feeling the English killer has been moonlighting north of the border. I'd prefer to use a policewoman, but I think it'd be better if I used your services. Our killer will be able to spot an undercover policewoman at one thousand yards. Don't ask why but they can always smell a copper. Using you also means I don't have to run it past my dog wanking superior Cruickshank, who's on my case night and day. Not that I have much choice. Elvis here told me in no uncertain terms I was only getting the photo of a suspicious car with the dodgy licence plate if you were both involved in the case.'

'That's all well and good, but what, exactly, is in it for me?' April asked.

'Well, maybe if you help catch one of the killers you'll keep your job,' Crosbie said.

'And …' April demanded.

'And … I'll run a background check on the Weasel for you. Deal?' he said hopefully.

'Ach, what else have I got to do with my time anyway? I'm suspended. And if I get the sack, at least I'll have a head start going on the game.'

42

CUT AND THRUST

The broom cupboard was pretty lonely without the constant chatter from across the desk. Connor missed April's ramblings. He could still recall a recent conversation about her kitchen saga. Before he had barely been able to take his coat off one morning, April had been in full flight. 'Do you know Liz Cowley from advertising? Of course you do, big, hefty lass with too much make-up. Well, her best friend Heather is going out with a joiner who's just got her pregnant. Well, I got him to fit my kitchen units, and what a mess, by the way. He's made a total pig's ear of it. Everything's skewiff.'

Connor had laughed as April retold this tale while wearing a pair of squint, mangled glasses she'd obviously sat on for the umpteenth time. 'Anyway,' she continued, barely pausing for breath, 'I went right through him for his shoddy workmanship, and do you know what he did?'

'Shat himself?' Connor asked hopefully.

'Almost as bad – he cried. Seriously, stood their bubbling like a big baby. I told him he'd need to pull himself together now he's going to be a dad. What a mess to get himself in getting Liz Cowley's best friend Heather pregnant and mucking up my kitchen units.'

The memory evaporated as the broom cupboard door flew open and the Weasel strode in. 'How's one half of Scotland's best crime-fighting duo this morning?'

'Fine,' Connor replied straight-faced, 'and how's Scotland best ever news editor?'

The Weasel chose not to reply to the quip. Instead, he hit Connor with his morning mantra of, 'What have you got for the schedule?'

'I could do you a cutts job on Scotland's unsolved murders if that's any use? Because apart from that I have nothing else on,' Connor smiled, just to make sure he got right up the Weasel's nose.

The news editor's beady little eyes narrowed. If Connor had been a junior reporter, he'd have bawled him out across the editorial floor and then called him at midnight to demand he do an early morning stakeout, a tactic he had used all too often to erode the fragile confidence of those starting out in the business. Instead he decided to bide his time and snapped, 'Cutts job it is, and since you've no real stories you can rewrite a press release, too,' before tossing a sheet of A4 onto Connor's desk.

Connor's heart sank. Press release rewrites were the bane of a journalist's life, usually government surveys or private sector research which tried to present itself as hard news facts in return for a plug in the paper. They were mostly dubious at best – the condom makers who claimed their brand was used more often in Scotland per head of population than anywhere else in the world. The helpful PRs even supplied headline suggestions, adjusted to the style of the papers they targeted, so the red tops would receive RANDY SCOTS ARE TOP OF THE BONKS while more upmarket publications would receive SCOTS ARE TOP OF THE LOVE LEAGUE.

It was all nonsense as far as Connor was concerned. But desk heads loved these press releases because they were cheap, filled a space and gave them something for their schedules. 'And they wonder why circulations are plummeting,' thought Connor. He turned to the copy and deliberately misspelled the name of the contraceptive brand throughout in the hope that it wouldn't get picked up by the subs and make it into the paper.

It had just gone 11 a.m. and he'd already done his work for the day. It would buy him some much needed time to execute the plan he had hatched with April and DCI Crosbie. But first he needed to visit an old friend.

April had decided to treat her daughter Jayne to lunch in Windows restaurant on the top floor of the Carlton George Hotel. April loved the place. It was so intimate and sunny, with views across George Square and the city's rooftops.

She had done many interviews there over the years, before the Weasel had banned 'entertaining' on expenses. That had been like having a limb cut off. If a journalist couldn't entertain on company expenses, then they were immediately at a disadvantage, as far as she was concerned. Sure, the system had been battered and abused over the years, mostly by newspaper executives who didn't think twice about adding bottles of champagne to the bill, but meanwhile foot soldiers like April sweated over ordering a couple of cappuccinos.

A good lunch never failed to get a good interview. When people were relaxed they revealed things they'd never told the press before.

Then there had been the time April had recommended this same hotel to the head PR at Camelot, who ran Britain's National Lottery. They would bring their jackpot winners to the boutique hotel to meet the press, and the PR would make sure she gave April a little titbit or two more that'd give her a better angle than the rest of the press pack.

April loved Lottery winners. Factory worker syndicates always looked so uncomfortable in their new suits and frocks, and whenever the photographers asked the winners to give a cheesy kick for the cameras, the labels from their newly purchased shoes would be clearly visible on the soles.

April often thought of journalism as acting. Each story was like a different role. One day it would be health, the next a death knock, or a showbiz sit down. The job certainly had its moments, but the highs were fewer and more far between than the day-to-day drudgery. She would be acting out a new role tonight and was beginning to feel a little anxious about her stint as a hooker. What if she was picked up by this psycho? What if he killed her? Crosbie had assured her she would be safe, but what if something went wrong? And what legacy would she leave behind if she were murdered? Would people say she'd been a good journalist but a bad mother?

That's why she had decided to call Jayne. After they had ordered, Jayne had asked her what was up. April had welled up and eventually told her daughter everything, from being suspended and how her mean bosses were trying to get rid of her on the cheap to tonight's dangerous mission. The two women had talked for hours, the first time they had spoken to each other so honestly and openly in years.

At the end of their lunch Jayne had kissed her mum and hugged her tightly. April Lavender no longer felt like a useless mother. Jayne had said, 'Sometimes we all just need a hug.'

April now had her fighting spirit back. And she was ready to catch a killer.

43

FAREWELL TO A FRIEND

Badger looked terrible. His face was gaunt and his skin so grey it was practically transparent. He was lying on top of his sheets, with a pair of paper trousers barely covering his modesty. His face lit up when he saw his protégé. He uttered, 'Elvis, how you doing?' before his voice was replaced by a hacking cough.

He wasn't able to speak again for several minutes. He tugged at the knees of his paper trousers. 'Pretty snazzy, eh? I was thinking of going jigging in them later on. Give it some of my John Travolta moves.' He was on a roll now. 'The beauty with these is, if you shit yersel, they just tear them off and give you a new pair. I wish I'd known about them years ago.'

They both laughed which sparked off another prolonged coughing fit for Badger. When his chest finally calmed down, they sat together with smiles on their faces.

It was Badger who spoke first. 'So, how's old April shaping up?'

'Not so great, Badg, but she's a tough old burd,' Connor told him before silence ensued again.

Badger sighed. 'Newspapers are not what they used to be, Elvis. I've worked under my fair share of editors, many of them drunks and hotheads, but, boy, they were good. They knew instinctively what their readers wanted, what was a *Daily Herald* story. They worked you hard but you always wanted to go the extra mile for them. And they'd always buy you a pint afterwards. But this new breed are not only vindictive, they're fucking hopeless. Can you imagine someone like Danny Brown treating April this way? No chance. If she fucked up, Danny would be the first to bollock her, but then that would've been it. End of story, the next day it would all be forgotten – the way it should be. Now we have a little cunt like the Weasel terrorising his staff, psychologically wearing the poor bastards down, going out of his way to end careers, and for what? His own pleasure, the twisted little fuck. I just can't understand their mentality. How does a frightened, demoralised staff produce exciting stories? They don't, then year in, year out the quality of the papers drops as fast as their circulation.'

Badger realised he was ranting and gave a shrug. Connor had a slightly more pragmatic view. He believed many journalists did have a sell-by date. He hated the old codgers kicking around newsrooms, boring everyone with their tales from their glory days. That sort of banter was fine for the boozer but not when everyone else was trying to work.

Badger had been different. He had continued to produce the same stunning range of stories and investigations until the day he'd been forcibly retired. He had called it his 'freelance mentality', explaining to Connor, 'Treat every working day as if you're a freelance – no stories, no pay. Too many of these staff cunts think they can cruise by on a story or two a week. Hell's teeth, in the old union days with overstaffing some writers didn't bother their typewriters for months on end. But who the hell wants to sit around doing nothing? Not me.'

He concluded their chat on an upbeat note. 'Look, the industry has changed. People now read their news on their bloody smartphones rather than on newsprint, but remember, Connor, good writing, however it's delivered, will never go out of fashion. And you're good. In fact, I don't think you know just how good you are. So don't let the bastards grind you down.'

With that he closed his eyes and fell asleep.

Connor kissed his mentor gently on the forehead and said his goodbyes for the last time.

DCI Crosbie was tentative when speaking to anyone now that his inner monologue was fully unleashed. He hoped for the sake of his career it would stay quiet while he spoke to his superior, Cruickshank.

'Making progress, Crosbie?' Cruickshank enquired.

'Yes, sir. Anticipating some developments tonight, sir,' he

replied, trying desperately to keep his answers as short and formal as was politely possible, in case any expletives escaped.

'Oh, Crosbie, just to let you know, if we don't see some positive results as you keep promising then DCI Creaney shall be taking over the case.'

Crosbie flinched at the mere mention of Creaney's name. In every area of working life, there is always someone you cannot stand the sight of and someone who feels exactly the same way about you. This was the case with Creaney and Crosbie.

Beads of sweat gathered on the detective's forehead as he struggled to contain the urge to give a full and frank account of what he thought about Creaney. Somehow he managed to keep his alter ego at bay. He'd got away with it. He really needed to take himself up a big mountain and scream obscenities at the top of his voice as Watt Wilson had recommended. That would give him renewed confidence about staying on top of his split personality.

However, Cruickshank was feeling a lot less confident about the investigation's progress as he left Crosbie's office. 'Unless I'm very much mistaken,' the DS later told the Chief Constable during a briefing, 'DCI Crosbie concluded our meeting by calling me a cocksucker.'

44

TO CATCH A KILLER

Connor and April entered DCI Crosbie's Pitt Street office to find the detective sitting behind his desk looking the perfect picture of authority – until he opened his mouth.

'It's fatso and cunty, how are you twatting on?' he said offering a friendly handshake.

'That doesn't even make sense,' Connor replied sternly, refusing to shake Crosbie's hand.

It was April who broke the tension. 'Now, now, David, remember what I said about keeping that potty mouth of yours under control. I think you need a few more sessions with Watt before you end up in hot water.'

'You're right,' he replied looking suitably chastised. 'You're cunting right as friggedy fuckety usual, cow face,' he added, realising with horror that he'd started making up swear words that he'd never heard of.

'You,' Connor growled, pointing directly at Crosbie, 'are a fucking nutter.'

Even Crosbie's inner self realised it had gone too far. He desperately tried to regain his composure. 'Okay, Miss Lavender, fancy being a washed-up old hooker tonight instead of a washed-up old hack?' The detective surprised himself with the last statement. He was pretty sure he'd made it himself, without the foul-mouthed interjection of his 'dark side'.

April considered her transformation into an old streetwalker. It had all been a bit too easy. The only major adjustment she'd made was to tie her hair back and put on a short summer skirt she hadn't worn in years, with a pair of high-heeled shoes. The plunging top was one she regularly wore on a rare night out. As for the make-up, there wasn't much extra she could slap on her face. Connor would joke how she virtually put the stuff on with a trowel anyway, the older and craggier she got.

Right now, she'd give anything not to be standing on a freezing street corner just off Blythswood Square. A couple of potential punters had just driven slowly by, inspecting the 'goods' and thought better of it despite April's best efforts to tempt them, leaning forward provocatively so that her ample chest nearly spilled out of her top. Each time a kerb crawler sped off she'd chuckle to herself ruefully, 'I can't even tempt the pervs any more.'

Crosbie's surveillance team were stationed directly opposite April's 'patch', with an officer happily photographing the number plates and occupants of every car that approached her. The two officers had been given an intense briefing by DCI Crosbie, who had strenuously warned them to be on full alert, saying, 'I want pictures of everyone, but even more importantly than that, do not, whatever you fucking do, cunting lose sight of April Lavender. We'll be in enough shite if this cocking operation goes tits and fanny up for using a civilian as bait in the arsing first place, never mind the pissing crap the *Daily Herald* will pour over us.'

The surveillance team had sat slack-jawed throughout Crosbie's expletive-ridden briefing. Afterwards one of them had remarked, 'Do you think he's alright? He doesn't half swear a lot.'

But they had remained alert as instructed, with the 35mm lens of a Nikon camera trained on April's feeble attempts to drum up custom. A bin lorry was slowly working its way down the road, warning lights flashing, while its 'sanitation officers' collected the blue wheelie bins stuffed full of paper for recycling from the numerous city centre offices. It wasn't long before the lorry's giant yellow frame filled the lens of the Nikon, as the bins were loaded and lifted mechanically, and the contents dumped into the rear of the machine. The lorry then rumbled on noisily.

The photographer put his eye to the viewfinder before gently swivelling it left and then right. He then peered out the back of the unmarked van with the one-way glass to look at April's street corner with the naked eye before turning to his colleague in a state of mild panic and swearing, 'Oh fuck – she's gone.'

45

RAW FEAR

April had known her fair share of men. She'd been married three times and had several lovers before, after and occasionally during her marriages. April had considered the Pill one of the greatest inventions ever made, believing the claims that it was empowering and had given women control of their bodies and their lives. But she would later scoff at these opinions. Women could still contract sexually transmitted diseases, many of which were far more serious for a woman than the male carrier.

It also didn't stop certain men from forcibly having sex when they wanted. Nowadays that was rightly called rape. But when April was first married it became a normal part of her relationship. Her husband would come back from the pub drunk, and whether April was sleeping or watching the telly, they would have sex. How did the Pill empower women to prevent that happening? The truth was, it didn't.

April began to think that the only people that the Pill truly benefited were men. She had sometimes been slightly scared when her first brutish husband had been in one of his moods. She could sense what was coming. Mercifully, he wouldn't hit her, although that was only after she learned not to resist. But the middle-aged man who had just picked her up truly terrified her. There was something primitive and powerful about his whole demeanour and even his musk.

He had been perfectly polite to begin with, explaining, 'I'm a stranger in this town, so I didn't know where to come, if you know what I mean. But then I saw you standing on the corner and thought, *bingo*! Yip, as soon as I set eyes on you, I said to myself, "So this is where they keep the disease-ridden, filthy old slags."'

His smile had remained fixed at first, making April wonder if she had really heard what he'd said. But she was left in no doubt, when he turned to face her while driving, with raw hatred in his eyes, and said coldly, 'I'm right, aren't I? You're a filthy old whore?'

April knew her 'client' was deliberately working himself up into a fury. She attempted to steer the conversation away from the dangerous ground it was heading and shrugged, saying mildly, 'Well, we've all got to earn a living, haven't we, love?'

The chummy chat wrong-footed Osiris momentarily before he regained his focus. He had expected April to be rigid with fear after his cold threat. All the others had been. Instead, she had acted as if she had misheard him at first – which wasn't uncommon where April was concerned – then nonchalantly given a banal response as if defending her profession on some tacky daytime talk show.

Osiris hadn't planned to take another victim. But, still excited by the thrill of leaving Martin Seth swinging from the rafters of his lodge, he simply couldn't suppress his bloodlust when he spotted the opportunity to pick up the ageing streetwalker.

The killer calmly took control of the steering wheel with his left hand, before throwing a short, powerful right jab across his body which caught April squarely on the jaw, instantly knocking her out.

Osiris said, 'Am I making myself loud and clear now, bitch? You are going to die.'

DCI Crosbie had also briefly lost sight of April as the bin lorry passed. But he had been quicker to respond than the surveillance unit, slipping his unmarked BMW into gear and moving into the unusually heavy traffic to follow the dark red Mondeo in front.

He could clearly see a blonde-haired woman in the passenger seat beside the male driver. 'I cunting know this is my motherfucker. Who else but a crazy serial killer prick would go to the red light cocksucking district when he knows the coppers will be trawling the joint?' Crosbie caught sight of his own gleeful expression in his rear-view mirror and moaned, 'I don't have a clue who I am any more.'

The man in the mirror smiled back. 'Don't worry arsehole – together we're going right to the top. Imagine the fucking fun, frolics and damage we could do as Chief Constable. Jeez, it'd be a laugh – and we'll get there by catching this twathead.'

Crosbie picked up his radio to speak to the controller, 'I need a number plate checked out. It's 'SC08 TWF – that's Shit Cunt Zero Eight Titty Wank Fuck. Did you get that?'

'Er, yes, DCI Crosbie,' replied a twitchy controller, 'we'll get that checked out right away.'

Connor was also finding the traffic tricky to negotiate. The *Daily Herald* photographer in the passenger seat urged the reporter to drive closer to the red Mondeo. 'Come on, Elvis, I can't get any snaps from this distance,' Jack Kennedy complained.

No matter how meticulous Crosbie, Connor and April had been plotting their streetwalker sting, it had still managed to implode over an unexpected bin lorry and heavy traffic from a concert at the Scottish Exhibition and Conference Centre.

Connor suddenly felt the need to quote the Bard, Rabbie Burns: 'The best-laid plans o' mice and men. Gang aft agley.'

DCI Crosbie had the Mondeo in his sights. After April had got in at Blythswood Square, the car had hung right into Hope Street and headed towards Charing Cross, where it could join the M8 motorway in either direction. Crosbie knew he'd need to have his wits about him. The traffic was almost gridlocked around the junctions thanks to the concert at SECC, with 8,000 music fans all heading over at the same time.

The red Mondeo was waiting at the lights. Crosbie focused on his prey as he sat just three cars behind. He could see the heads angled slightly towards each other – maybe April was still negotiating a price. 'Or maybe the dirty bastard is trying to get some discount after seeing the goods.'

Crosbie's alter ego let out a cackle that made his skin crawl. His inner self both appalled and impressed him. He hated his callousness but loved his confidence. He could actually feel the self-belief coursing through his veins when his alter ego asserted himself. It felt dangerous but invigorating at the same time – as if he could tackle anything.

Right now he was confident he had a serial killer in his sights. This was a murderer of prostitutes the length and breadth of the UK – someone who had always managed to evade the long arm of the law since god knows when. It just had to be him. The car's description matched the grainy photo supplied by the cousin of April's friend. This multiple murderer would be unable to ignore his urge to kill. DCI David 'Bing' Crosbie finally had him in his sights.

'You won't be a DCI for much longer when you feel this cunt's collar,' his inner self cackled once more. But, like many over-confident people, Crosbie's split personality was also arrogant.

His smile cracked when the Mondeo suddenly indicated and pulled out of the queue of traffic for the motorway. He had no choice but to break cover and follow the target along Argyle Street into Anderston district, where the car indicated right and performed a U-turn. Any last pretence of following discreetly would be blown if Crosbie performed the same manoeuvre. Instead, he waited until the car passed him on the opposite side of the road, when he took a very clear mental picture of the driver, before performing his own U-turn and following.

The target was driving back towards Blythswood Square. Maybe he wasn't horny any more after just five minutes in April's company. Crosbie scoffed, 'I know how you feel, pal.' He reckoned listening to the ageing hack prattling on would have the most law-abiding person in a homicidal rage. 'Come on, man – don't chicken out. Do her!' Crosbie screamed at his windscreen. He could still bring him in for soliciting even if he didn't actually attack April.

The Mondeo pulled up outside the plush boutique hotel Malmaison on West George Street. Alarm bells started ringing in Crosbie's ears. 'This can't be right – no murderer would take a manky old hooker into such a posh hotel.'

Crosbie parked across the street just as the driver stepped out of his car. He was tall, well built, wearing jeans, a bomber jacket and trainers more suited to a man at least half his age. His frame obscured Crosbie's view of April as she got out of the car. A concierge appeared as the driver shouted in a loud American accent, 'Jeez, buddy, this place is hard to find, especially when you make me drive on the wrong side of the road.'

Crosbie felt sick to the pit of his stomach. The big Yank moved to the boot of the car to retrieve his luggage, giving Crosbie a clear view of his passenger. The peroxide hair and stature were all the same – but it was most definitely not April Lavender.

46

DEATH BECOMES HER

After gagging April and restraining her hands behind her back with plastic ties, Osiris had heaved her unconscious, bound body into the back seat of the Mondeo. He had ripped open her blouse and pulled up her bra. 'Just look at your saggy old tits. You disgust me,' he snarled, before slapping her hard with the back of his hand.

The car was parked in a deserted street in Glasgow's Kinning Park, outside a plumber's merchant. He had chosen his spot days previously, noting how the street had little traffic, no CCTV and was long enough to easily spot anyone approaching at a distance in either direction.

Satisfied he had prepped properly, he congratulated himself on following his American life guru's advice to the letter. 'Make a plan, work out every little detail and just do it, people! What are you waiting for? Do it, do it, do it!' The studio crowd had reached fever pitch, screaming, 'DO IT! DO IT! DO IT!'

If only they all knew what they were just about to encourage Osiris to do.

He ripped April's underwear off. The reporter came to, with fear and confusion in her eyes. Osiris was unbuckling his trousers. He grabbed her painfully by the throat and told her, 'I am going to fuck you and kill you at the same time, you fat old whore.' He smashed his fist into April's face, before punching her body repeatedly.

The pain was excruciating. April could hardly breathe. She knew death was upon her.

Suddenly, a female voice shouted, 'Aye, that's the cunt, alright!' before 50,000 volts from a Taser stun gun coursed through Osiris's body. He had never felt pain like it before. After the sharp jolt the killer lay paralysed and helpless as his hands and feet were bound with plastic ties, similar to the ones he'd so often used on his own victims.

Osiris was then hauled to his feet by three men the size of gorillas. He looked at the face he'd just smashed to a pulp in his red Mondeo. Blood was splattered all over the inside of the windows. His victim had been a gusher, probably because she was on medication for high blood pressure, he guessed. It had happened to him before with the older ones.

Scottish newspaper legend April Lavender was now barely recognisable. Her battered and bruised body lay crumpled in the back of Osiris's car.

A whiny female voice said, 'Look at the state of that poor auld burd. That's whit he'd huv dun tae me, the fucking beast. I hope youse fuck him up good.'

In what felt like slow motion Osiris turned his head and managed to focus on the source of the most guttural Glaswegian accent he'd ever heard – which was quite something in a city where it seemed everyone spoke their own version of English. It was a girl. Or, to be more accurate, the prostitute who had given him oral sex two nights previously, before he'd stuffed money into her mouth and chucked her out the car.

She looked at him with pure venom in her eyes, then hawked up something from the deepest regions of her throat and spat in Osiris's face. 'Aye, that's the cunt, alright.'

Osiris needed to focus. What would his self-help guru say now? 'Evaluate the situation then rise above your problems. Only then will everything come clearly into focus.' But everything was already clearly in focus, and Osiris didn't like what he saw. He could not turn his head far enough to the side to see the slabs of muscle holding him upright. For whenever he tried to move, they tightened their grip. He knew any notion of escape was futile. Even if he managed to break free they'd zap him with that Taser again.

Then, a much smaller figure emerged from the shadows, his face partially illuminated by the cigarette burning in his mouth. Although around half the size of the men who were gripping

Osiris with their shovel-sized hands, the man who approached looked somehow more intimidating. Osiris's deep animal instincts could sense danger.

The mysterious figure got so close Osiris could feel his hot breath on his cheeks. Then he spoke, 'So you're the guy who murdered my sister?'

Osiris gave an involuntary shrug. It could be any number of victims this cool customer was talking about.

Colin Harris said, 'Not too bothered? Oh, you will be. The thing is, you may have been able to give the cops and the reporters the slip, but not me, pal. Takes a killer to know a killer.'

Harris produced a knife, and held it glinting in the moonlight.

Just the sight of it made Osiris Vance, mass murderer, terroriser and killer of women the length and breadth of Britain, copiously urinate himself. This was true fear. He could feel the same panic he used to see in his victims' faces.

He was dragged to a waiting car and sandwiched in the back seat between the two gorillas.

Harris threw his cigarette butt into the bushes and took his place in the driver's seat, joined in the front by the girl. He calmly handed the prostitute a thick envelope and said, 'That's £100,000. Enough money for you to get clean, off the streets and start a new life with your kid, okay?' A part of Colin Harris genuinely wished she would start afresh, but he knew it was more likely she'd waste it all on heroin, bought from his suppliers, and probably be dead within weeks.

That was the last humanitarian thought Harris would have that night. His mind turned to much darker matters as he glanced towards Osiris in his rear view mirror.

47

BUSTED FLUSH

Osiris decided to use the only trump card he had left. 'I know who killed that rich bitch, Selina Seth.'

Harris scoffed, 'What, poor Martin? No wonder he killed her, she was screwing anything that moved. Tormented him over it, too. I told him he should just admit it. He'd easily have got a diminished responsibility rap. Seven years for manslaughter. Out in three and a half. Then the daft bastard killed himself ... or was it made to look like suicide?'

A thought suddenly occurred to Harris, 'Maybe you had a hand in that too? Probably thought you were onto a good thing, eh? Maybe you decided to blackmail him so you'd end up on the company payroll? That well and truly fucked up one of my better business plans, so that's something else I owe you.'

'No, not him. It wasn't Martin who killed Selina,' Osiris protested.

Harris was silent for a long time, as he listened to what Osiris had to say. Eventually he said, 'Interesting, very interesting,' his mind already whirring at the possibilities of how best to use this new crucial information.

Sensing a bargaining tool, Osiris continued, 'He's crazy. I've seen him in action. He set about that rich cow like a maniac.'

Harris scoffed, 'At least he's smarter than you. You've just shown your hand. Cashed in your chips, buddy. You have nothing else in the kitty.'

The colour drained from Osiris face as the realisation set in – he'd blown it. He should have bargained for his life with the only piece of information he had left. Instead, he'd given it up all too willingly. It was only then that Osiris realised his self-help gurus had been a complete waste of his time and money.

They did nothing but spout clichés, bluff and hot air, and only benefited the gurus themselves. Like leaders of some religious cult they sold ideas to the needy and the weak-minded, like snake oil salesmen of old.

Harris's car came to a halt in a darkened street. Moments later the goons hauled Osiris from the back seat. 'Fancy a drink?' Harris said with a sinister smile as Osiris was frogmarched through the entrance of the Portman bar. The trap door to the cellar was already open, and the last of the regulars were stumbling out at closing time. No one even gave Harris and his men a second look. They knew better.

The gruff barmaid was collecting the last of the glasses. She asked Harris if he wanted a glass of his usual Chablis.

'Aye, better make it the whole bottle, darling. And my blow-torch too, honey. It's going to be a long night.' He gave her a friendly wink.

Harris turned to face Osiris and lit the nozzle of the blowtorch with a lighter, adjusting the sputtering yellow flame to an angry-looking blue point. 'Now, how do you like your genitals? Well done? Or burnt to a crisp? I think we'll go for the latter, shall we?'

48

CARRY ON LIVING

April could hear the voices in her head. Barely audible at first, they were growing louder and louder, and they were talking about her.

'The big yin'll be raging she's missed her breakfast again.'

'Aye, she's fading away tae a mountain.'

She didn't recognise her mockers. Who were they? And more to the point where the hell was she? She managed to open her eyes for a brief moment.

One of the voices spoke again. 'She's awake, better get the nurse.'

Nurse. Hospital. Wards. April's mind wandered. She thought of her favourite *Carry On* film: Kenneth Williams fending off the attentions of Hattie Jacques, an even larger lady than herself, and a craggy-faced Sid James in constant pursuit of sexy nurse Barbara Windsor. April remembered getting into a heated argument with her friend Flo, who'd insisted the films were nothing but sexist old drivel and complained that the Royal College of Nursing was still trying to rid itself of Barbara's image forty years on.

Why did people have to dissect everything? April wondered. And why was she in hospital? She remembered speaking to Detective Crosbie, then pulling on clothes which were far too tight for her and finally Connor wishing her luck. But wishing her luck for what?

April broke out in a cold sweat and her heart began to race, sounding off some alarm by the side of her bed. Another voice filled her head that made her jump: 'I'm going to fuck you and kill you.' Her arms flayed wildly and she let out a long, anguished scream.

'You're all right, Miss Lavender, you're safe now. You're safe.'

April opened her tear-filled eyes to see a sweet, young nurse smiling down at her. 'Am I . . . did he . . .' she stuttered, before breaking down in gut-wrenching sobs.

'I'll get the doctor to speak to you,' the nurse said before she whispered in April's ear, 'but, no, he didn't. You had a lucky escape.'

It was all April wanted to know. Whoever he was had beaten her badly but by some miracle hadn't raped her. Lucky escape? April pondered. There was no way she could have escaped given the state she'd been in. She shut her eyes tightly and thought hard. Plastic ties had been around her wrists. She remembered the searing pain of being repeatedly punched in the face, the smell of coffee and stale cigarettes on her attacker's breath, and his powerful hands ripping at her clothes before tightening around her throat. Then there had been a jolt, like an electric shock. Voices. Different voices. And that was all she could recall.

'Good morning, April. I'm Doctor Crawford.'

April looked up to see another fresh-faced young woman who wouldn't have looked out of place in a school uniform.

'You know you're getting old when the doctors and nurses look so young,' April croaked.

'Well, it's nice to finally meet you,' the doctor said, pulling up a chair. 'You've been staying with us for a couple of nights, so it's good to hear you talk, however you sound.'

'I sound bloody awful,' April said. 'Like I've smoked a thousand fags.'

'I'm not surprised. You've had a fair bit of trauma to your head and neck. There's still quite a lot of bruising, so you might not want to enter any beauty pageants for a while.'

April liked this doctor. 'Do you know what happened? And where am I, incidentally?'

Doctor Crawford apologised. 'Sorry, I should've said. You're in the Royal Infirmary. But as for what happened we don't really know a lot yet. You came in as an emergency. Someone called 999 and you were found in a car. That's the sum of my knowledge, I'm afraid. But the police can tell you more.' The doctor glanced towards the door.

April narrowed her eyes, attempting to focus without the aid of her glasses. She could make out a uniformed policeman standing outside her room. 'I take it my attacker hasn't been caught?' she asked gloomily.

The doctor shrugged. 'I don't know. What I can tell you for certain is you're going to be all right. You've been through the wringer, but the X-rays show nothing's broken. And there are no signs of sexual assault.'

'Not for a long time,' April joked, trying to bluff her obvious relief. Her eyes settled on a nearby table festooned with Get Well Soon cards and bouquets of flowers. She reached out and picked up the nearest one, recognising Connor's scrawl. 'Being choked half to death is no excuse for not filing your copy on time.'

'Cheeky bastard, but he does make me smile,' April said.

The policeman opened the door to announce, 'You have a visitor, Miss Lavender.'

'Talk of the devil,' April croaked.

'My, what a lovely singing voice you have!' Connor quipped, placing a tinfoil-covered plate on the table beside her. 'I thought I better buy you something from Peccadillos. They've nearly gone out of business since you've been in here.'

The doctor excused herself.

Connor slumped into the chair and moaned, 'Jeez, between you and Badger, I feel like I'm never away from hospitals.'

'How is he?' April asked.

'Ach, not great. Rita's been texting me, but he could go at any minute. With all that's happened I haven't really had a chance to see him again,' Connor said quietly.

'He'd understand more than anyone – the story always comes first,' April assured him.

'Anyway, how are you feeling?' Connor said.

'I'm fine. Just pleased to be here.'

'Jayne's practically been keeping a bedside vigil, but you've been out of it, snoring your head off as usual. And everyone at work has been asking for you.' Connor smiled.

Not everyone, I bet, April thought to herself, with the mere mention of work blackening her mood. She shuddered at the humiliation of being suspended by the Weasel. 'Just look at the state of me, Connor. Beaten to a pulp trying to save my job. And where did it get me? A hospital bed and police protection from some lunatic trying to bump me off.'

'Actually, I've just heard some news on that front. Our killer's bumping-off days are firmly behind him.'

But the news of Osiris's death fell on deaf ears. 'I'll be out of work shortly and probably dead a few years after that and I'll ask myself, What the hell was all that about? Soon no one will even remember me. Maybe a great-great-grandchild will be a writer one day and her parents won't even know it was in her DNA. And even if someone does recall me, what's my legacy? A trail of broken marriages. Oh, and a serial killer almost strangled her to death. Big wow, huh?'

'Come on, April, you've had an incredible career. And it was your bravery that helped to catch the crazy bastard. And what about Jayne? What about your grandkid? You're lucky to have a legacy like them to leave behind.'

But April was having none of it. 'And as for newspapers, they're doomed – yesterday's news printed on dead trees. Soon people won't even believe they were bought in their millions every day. They're finished, Connor. The internet wins. And I'm finished, too. It's someone else's turn to toil.'

Connor let her get the rant out of her system, before appealing to the part of April he knew he could get through to – her stomach. 'So, are you going to eat this or what?' he said peeling back the tinfoil from the plate. 'I asked Martel to make you the lunchtime special. Two Scotch pies and beans, especially for you.'

April's mood instantly lightened. 'Well . . . it does smell marvellous.'

Connor watched with morbid fascination as she tucked into the pies. 'It's just gone nine and here you are having lunch. You're as happy as a pig in shit, aren't you?'

His words went off like a firecracker in April's head, forcing her to drop her knife and fork on the table. 'Nine o'clock? Lunch? That bastard didn't meet her for lunch the day before she was murdered. He met her the morning she *was* murdered.'

Connor knew April well enough to expect the unexpected, but the sudden outburst even wrong-footed him. He looked puzzled.

'Don't you know what this means?' April asked rhetorically, her voice growing in volume and confidence. 'It means I'm not the one who's finished. He is.'

Connor stared at April. 'Have you had a wee stroke this morning?'

'Ooh, matron,' she replied in her best Kenneth Williams's voice, 'I haven't had a wee stroke in years.'

THROWING OUT THE TRASH

April gingerly entered Bent's office without knocking. Her right arm was in a sling, and her face was still puffy and bruised after her brutal attack. She had spent just four days in hospital as her injuries had been mostly flesh wounds with no bones broken. The doctor had told her that her 'excess baggage' had saved her from any real damage – a polite way of saying she was fat. April had beamed when Connor came to visit her that night saying, 'Ha! Who said over-eating is bad for you?'

Bent was clearly in the middle of a personal call, feet up on the table, a rosy glow to his cheeks, and speaking in hushed, flirtatious tones. April thought the editor looked like a dirty sleazebag. He looked up, and immediately swung his feet off the desk, like a teenager caught with their trainers on their mum's coffee table. Or a man who'd just been caught red-handed flirting with another man's wife, which was probably more accurate. His tone changed. 'I'll call you back, something's come up.'

Bent regained his composure and glowered, 'If you need to see me, you should make an appointment with Grace.'

'Ah, and I distinctly recall you saying you were the "my door's always open" type when you arrived here,' April said coolly as she took a seat opposite him.

'I've been wanting to speak to you anyway,' Bent replied, trying to regain the upper-hand. 'I'm thinking that the long love affair between you and the *Daily Herald* has come to a natural conclusion. Even though you sustained injuries while on suspension, I have still decided to put together a compromise deal, which I hope you find acceptable,' he added with a smirk, failing to enquire how April was keeping since the attack and knowing that his compromise deal fell well short of any redundancy package she would be due after such long service.

He continued with an idle threat, 'It'd also save you leaving here with nothing, if the disciplinary panel found in our favour.'

'That doesn't bother me at the moment,' April lied. 'Right now I want to speak about another love affair, the one between you and Selina Seth.'

'What did you just say?' Bent growled, gripping the sides of the desk until his knuckles turned white.

'Please spare me the mock outrage,' April replied with composure. 'You were with her the morning of her death. In fact, you were there in the car park with her. You were the last one to see her alive. You withheld vital information to help catch her killer, but like a coward you kept quiet to protect your own name and your precious career.' April's voice grew louder and louder. 'You've been withholding information from a major murder inquiry. Yet all the time you and your attack dog saw fit to have me on some trumped-up charge just because I had a crisis of confidence. There is no way back for you now, Bent. Not only will you have to leave this newspaper, I'd leave the country if I were you. Blocking a police inquiry is still a serious offence in anyone's book – no matter how important you think you are.'

Like the thousands of articles she'd penned over her thirty-year career, April knew when to stop, but not before delivering her stinging pay-off line. 'Put it this way, Bent, if you don't leave my newspaper I'll make sure Mrs Bent and all the little Bent children know what a sleazy, spineless coward you really are. I think I've made myself clear.'

Bent slowly picked up a letter from his desk, and stared at it for a moment. Eventually, he said, 'I was going to turn this down. It's a formal job offer for a deputy editor post at the *Toronto Star*. Didn't really fancy the cold. But it suddenly seems a lot more appealing now.'

'I'm sure it does,' April said. 'And I think you should take your news editor, too. A man on the make in a new country will need a loyal lieutenant.' She hated to impose the Weasel on other journalists in another country, but experience had taught her that their type usually got their comeuppance.

April rose. It took some effort with the pain she was still in. She hobbled out without saying another word, leaving Nigel Bent to clear his desk.

Later that day April sat in Luigi's restaurant in front of a steaming, oversized bowl of pasta and meatballs, done in a tomato and roasted garlic sauce. It was delicious.

Luigi fussed over his favourite customer. 'Here-a, I have-a bib for you – I don't-a want-a you making a mess of such a lurv-erly blouse,' he said, tying a knot in a starched white napkin behind April's neck, before patting it flat down her ample bosom, letting his hands linger too long as usual.

April knew his game alright, but let it go. She was too hungry and sore to protest.

'Now-a, have you thought-a about my proposal,' Luigi asked, his bushy eyebrows arched in anticipation.

April gave him the brush off. 'I haven't had time to think of anything, Luigi. As you can see, I've been busy.'

'Well-a, my-a proposal still stands-a. You need-a someone to look-a after you. To keep you safe from the mad-a-men. You only have to say-a the word and it shall-a be done,' he said before disappearing off to another table.

April looked at Luigi's squat, chubby figure oozing out in all directions from under his kitchen whites. There was a time she wouldn't have looked twice at an old lech like him. But then again, that was when she was young, svelte and pretty. She looked down at the makeshift bib that Luigi had fashioned for her, now splattered with tomato and roasted garlic sauce. Her flabby belly was in three folds, two of them resting on the table.

She glanced at her reflection in the restaurant window and saw only an old woman looking back, with a ridiculous mop of harsh yellow hair. It would have been enough to put many women off their food, but not April. Eating and drinking were all she had left now she wasn't *officially* allowed to smoke any more.

Maybe she should just give in. She wouldn't just be marrying an old Italian; she would be marrying a great cook. They could grow old and fatter together. She would never have to worry about her backside being as wide as the Clyde, as Connor had once put it. And she'd have a companion. Maybe they'd even be happy together. It would certainly give Jayne one almighty shock. She could see her daughter's look of disapproval right now. 'Married? Having sex at your age? It's disgusting.'

'Yes, I plan on having lots of disgusting sex,' she chuckled to herself a little too loudly, catching the attention of some nearby diners and the proprietor.

'Hey, what-a you find-a so funny? You laughing at Luigi's meatballs?'

The image made them both laugh.

With a snap of Luigi's fingers, a young waiter brought April another bowl of meatballs to replace the empty one while Luigi topped up her glass of Chianti. He then grasped her hands tightly and said, 'You make-a my heart sing-a, April, because my-a food make-sa you so happy.'

She couldn't help noticing how his hands once again 'accidentally' brushed against her nipples. It felt quite nice, really. Maybe she would marry the old lech, after all …

50

VISITING AN OLD FRIEND

The next few days passed in a blur. April eventually wearied of all the congratulatory messages and calls of concern she had taken from her colleagues over the attack by Osiris and the sudden departure of Nigel Bent, who had been followed sharply out the door by his equally loathed news editor, the Weasel.

'What the fuck did you say to him?' Connor had asked with a mixture of admiration and wonder.

'The truth, Connor, just the truth. I always find that does wonders in my line of work.'

'But how did you know?' Connor asked still amazed.

'It suddenly came to me lying in my hospital bed. Bent was twitchy as hell because he hadn't met Selina for lunch the day before. He'd met her the morning she was murdered. I also had a very good source,' April said feeling pleased with herself.

'Who?' Connor asked.

'Now, now you know a good journalist never reveals their sources,' she replied with a sly smile.

'Yeah, but who said you were a good journalist?' Connor quipped.

'I asked his secretary Grace. We're old smoking buddies. She confirmed he hadn't been to lunch with anyone the previous day but had been unusually late on the morning of Selina's death.

'So I took a gamble and fronted him up. I just did my job basically.'

April wondered how she had managed to work full-time for most of her adult life. There didn't seem to be enough hours in the day. Like most folk in their fifties, she had begun to dream of the Utopia of retirement. Taking time to really browse through the shelves of IKEA. Leisurely weekday lunches instead of just at the weekend. Visiting the Burrell Collection – a museum she had lived nearby for the last twenty-five years but never once stepped foot in. But between the constant phone calls from her colleagues and her ardent suitor she didn't seem to have any time for herself.

Today would be different. She would make the time to visit Watt Wilson. She knew he was an old chancer, but he had the patter and the ability to make April, and his clients, feel a lot better on the way out his door than when they stepped in. In truth, she thought, therapists told you what you already knew. If you were overweight, it was because you put too much in and didn't burn up enough. But somehow listening to someone give you a rationale for binge eating – stress at work, relationships and so on – shifted some of the blame, so it wasn't entirely your fault.

April liked that about Watt. Of course, she also had an ulterior motive. Being a busybody, she wanted to ask Watt how he was getting on treating DCI Crosbie's Tourette's. Normal doctors would have been bound by the Hippocratic oath, but Watt wasn't even a doctor. He just acted like one, as if it was another role from his failed stage career.

She had tried calling ahead, but she kept getting his answering machine, which was so full it had stopped taking messages. April thought it strange he hadn't returned her calls – he always had before. She was pretty sure Watt had a little crush on her, or he had twenty years ago when she was a lot slimmer and better looking. She decided to pay him a personal visit instead, which would give her the motivation to get dressed today.

She pulled on her trousers and blouse, both of which felt tight, and let out a moan. 'I've just bought these and they're already too small.' She left the house in a glum mood. Hopefully, the old mind man would make her feel better.

April arrived at his door twenty minutes later and rang the bell. There was no reply. She didn't know why she did it – instinct, she would later guess – but after trying the front door, which was locked, she peered through Watt's ground-floor window.

His front room doubled as his therapy room, and as she shaded her eyes from the sunlight, she was able to focus on its dimly lit interior. There was Watt's well-worn couch, which April had lain on periodically over the last two decades. She then let out a small but clearly audible gasp as she spotted the twisted, bloodied and battered figure, which lay motionless and quite dead on top of it.

Watt would not be helping out April, or anyone else for that matter, ever again.

51

BLACK & WHITE

Always eager and keen to learn, the young PC on guard duty at Watt Wilson's front door asked his sergeant who was the DCI assigned to the murder case.

The old copper began singing in a sweet voice that belied his gruff looks, 'I'm dreaming of a white Christmas.'

The young PC looked utterly mystified.

Slightly annoyed with his underling's lack of musical knowledge, the older cop said, 'Bing Crosby, son? *White Christmas*? Bob Hope? All the great black-and-white movies they did? *Road to Bali*. Ah, Jeez, son, he's only the greatest singer who ever lived. Sinatra wasn't fit to lace his shoes.'

The young PC's brain was tied up in knots. His utter confusion showed in his vacant expression.

The sergeant swore under his breath, then as if speaking to a child, said loudly and slowly, 'I'll spell it out for you. The guy we're getting today is Bing Crosbie.'

The young PC had barely understood anything his old sergeant, who clearly liked a drink, had been banging on about. Was he really saying a famous singer would be investigating this murder case? He thought to himself that the old boy had flipped his lid.

DCI David 'Bing' Crosbie had overheard their entire conversation as he approached the murder scene. It was now impossible for him to differentiate between the good and bad side of his split personality, but he clearly heard one of the voices inside his head say, 'I don't know about *White Christmas*, but this murder investigation is going to be one big wanking whitewash.' He began happily humming the tune to the old festive favourite. There was a spring in his step as there was now no conflict in his mind whatsoever.

For evil had overcome good. His bad side had won the internal power struggle and was now fully in control of this fiercely ambitious DCI who was determined to rise through the ranks.

He stepped jauntily over the threshold into Watt Wilson's house where he found the old stage hypnotist exactly where he had left him three days before. He remembered in minute detail how the old ham had pleaded with him for his life, before desperately trying to defend himself by striking the detective with the silver pocket watch he had kept on a chain for over thirty years.

It was now in the possession of the murderer. Crosbie checked the time on Watt's prized watch, which he now kept in his top pocket, as he stood overlooking his victim's body.

The forensic team gathering evidence in Watt's front room would collect a small DNA sample that would perfectly match that of DCI Crosbie. It would later be dismissed as erroneous after Crosbie's assignation to investigate Watt's murder. He would receive a verbal rebuke from his superior DS Cruickshank for contaminating a crime scene for which Crosbie would apologise profusely then mutter under his breath, 'You don't know the half of it, dickhead.'

In a few months' time he would receive a promotion for his work in solving the murder of Selina Seth, concluding that her late husband Martin had killed her after witnessing his wife having sex with persons unknown. Crosbie had managed to convince his superiors to take the 'theoretically possible' option, that the widower had committed suicide, from Martin Seth's autopsy report. Eager to bring the high profile case to a speedy conclusion, they readily agreed.

In actual fact, Crosbie had killed Selina. Aroused by watching her liaison with cheating *Daily Herald* editor Nigel Bent, he had approached Selina on her way back to her own car and asked if she fancied another shag. She had looked him up and down and dismissed him with the remark, 'Well, certainly not with you again – I only shagged you last time to get off with my speeding ticket.'

It had been Crosbie who had pulled Selina over all those years ago, and it had been Crosbie who later had sex with her in the back of her Jaguar in the Lidl car park. He recalled how his uniform had turned Selina on and how she had even insisted he wear his hat as they 'did it'. He had been fixated with her ever since that moment.

In his head, she'd held a candle for him after all this time. He'd followed Selina in his spare time, like an obsessed stalker, and watched how she would wine and dine with powerful businessmen before disappearing off to expensive hotels to spend the night. But finally witnessing 'his Selina' have sex with another man then so ruthlessly reject his advances, as if he had meant nothing to her, had been too much to bear.

His attack on her had been a crime of passion. He was a man whose love for Selina had been a one-way street, just like her husband's Martin, on whom, with no remorse, he would later pin the crime.

Crosbie had wrapped up his next case when he found the mutilated body of Osiris Vance, which forensics confirmed was linked to the death of the streetwalker Jackie McIvor. Osiris was also wanted in connection with a dozen other cases of murdered prostitutes in England and Wales, dating back to the 1970s. He had killed twenty-one women in his lifetime, but he would only be linked officially to half that number. The total fell well short of Osiris's ambition to be the UK's most prolific serial killer. That dubious honour would remain with Doctor Harold Shipman, who murdered over two hundred of his patients.

Osiris's family chose to cremate the killer. Ironically, something similar had already happened to his genitals, which the autopsy report had simply stated as 'missing'.

Hiding in the shadows as usual, the serial killer had witnessed DCI Crosbie's violent attack on Selina. His ego had got the better of him, and the copycat killing of Jackie McIvor had been his downfall. Osiris had bargained neither on Selina's killer being a psychotic, high-ranking police officer nor on Jackie's brother being far more intelligent, dangerous and ruthless than he could ever hope to be.

Crosbie had received a tip-off about where to find Osiris's body from one Colin Harris, who also had a number of other interesting propositions for the rising DCI that he could hardly refuse. Harris knew Crosbie had murdered Selina Seth, and he had the DCI in his back pocket … for now.

Crosbie had crossed a line. He could never go back to being his old pathetic, insecure self. That man was dead. The DCI felt reborn. And this time he was ready to have some fun with his newfound lease of life.

EPILOGUE

April had promised herself she wouldn't do it. In fact, she had promised several people, including her eternally disapproving daughter. But as she stood sheltered from the elements in a cigarette butt-littered lane outside the *Daily Herald*, she lit up and drew deeply on her Menthol Light. It felt like the embrace of an old friend.

Four whole years of being an ex-smoker had gone up in a puff of smoke.

The world had changed since April had last smoked. There was now a smoking ban in public places, which meant smokers now huddled in groups outside their favourite pubs and restaurants like social lepers. But the lure had always been there, pulling April in like a magnetic force, until she could resist no more.

She could almost hear in her mind the interminable lecture Jayne would give her if she was ever caught. She already had her excuses ready. Being attacked by Osiris ... Discovering Watt's dead body ... Not to mention the stress of being suspended, confronting her boss and seeing two of the most hated men in the *Daily Herald*'s history off the premises.

But in truth April began smoking again because it made her feel very, very naughty – like a teenager again.

'Hey, maybe smoking will help me lose some of this excess weight I've been carting around,' she said aloud. She took another deep drag, savouring every moment, before staring at the glowing tip of her cigarette.

There had been a time when April had smoked at her desk, with an overflowing ashtray spilling over everything. With hundreds of hacks puffing away at the same time, it had been hard to see from one end of the newsroom to the other through the fug of smoke.

'Imagine that now?' She laughed to no one in particular. 'Smoking at your desk? You'd be frogmarched out the building.'

Even when the company had built an ultra-modern, steel and glass, air-conditioned office block next to their crumbling old one, staff were still allowed to smoke at their desks, such was the power of their unions. But when the government's smoking ban was finally made law, smokers were banished outdoors to converted bus shelters that did little to protect them from the relentless Scottish weather.

April smoked her ciggie right down to the butt then crushed it under the ball of her foot. She took great pleasure swivelling her shoe from side to side as she mashed the evidence into the ground. But her moment of immense self-satisfaction was short-lived.

With a heavy heart, April made her way slowly back to her office, her wide hips swaying from side to side like a duck's bottom. For the second time in recent memory Scottish newspaper legend April Lavender had gone to work wearing a pair of mismatched shoes.